"By the time I met Clara, ordinary sexual relations were a rather tedious appetizer for her. It was the variation that counted. She could go to bed with a dozen men, one after the other, or all at once, and still not find the thrill she was looking for."

"And what was the thrill?"

He shrugged. "When one is as debauched as she was, can there be any thrills left? Well, whatever sensations the body can experience, Clara experienced."

Other books by
ALIZARIN LAKE

Business as Usual
Diary of an Angel
Festival of Venus
The Erotic Adv. of Harry Temple
More Erotic Adv. of Harry Temple

CLARA

ALIZARIN LAKE

MASQUERADE BOOKS, INC.
801 SECOND AVENUE
NEW YORK, N.Y. 10017

CHAPTER ONE

I.

One morning in the spring of 1953, almost all the Paris dailies ran headline stories of the "strange and violent death of Baroness Clara Arvon." It is, of course, part of a newspaper's business to run stories about strange and violent death. Generally all the brutal details are itemized—the blood, rape, murder, catastrophe pour out at us from the unemotional lines of black and white.

In the case of Baroness Arvon, her "strange and violent death" remained just that. The nude body of this remarkably beautiful woman had been found in a filthy (but unnamed) hotel in the Paris slum area. The proprietor of the hotel, when questioned by the police, said the woman had rented the room only a few hours before she was discovered dead. She had not filled out registration papers, the proprietor admitted, because she had claimed to be very tired when taking the room and said she would see to all the formalities when she went out for dinner. She never went out. At midnight, the proprietor knocked at her door and, since there was no answer, turned the knob and found that the door had not been locked from the inside. Baroness Arvon lay on the floor, an alcohol burner still sputtering on the table beside the bed.

I report the story of her death in almost the same words as the newspapers. The rest of the great amount of space devoted to Clara Arvon related the calm, quiet, virtuous events of her life. Born to middle-class parents, she had married at a very young age the formidable Baron Arvon, a man more than thirty years her senior, a man driven by bitterness and hatred because revolution had forced him from his own middle-European country to take up residence in France. Their marriage was a happy one (said the newspapers), but short-lived, since the Baroness was made a widow only four years after she had been made a bride. Left with a three-year-old daughter and several billion francs, Clara Arvon spent the second twenty years of her life in nun-like seclusion, emerging into society for a rare evening with intimate friends—usually Central European exiles—or, more frequently, for an afternoon devoted to some charitable benefit. Her good works were as great, and as little known, as her superlative beauty. Few indeed were those fortunate enough to behold this tall, slender woman with ice-blue eyes and ice-blue hair.

In short, nothing in her brief, quiet life—curiously enough, she died on her fortieth birthday—would have led anyone to expect she herself had, in a way, prophesied such a death. The newspapers reported that several of her intimates had informed the police that during the past year or two Baroness Arvon had often said, but always in jest, "One day I'll surprise all of you. I know you call me Baroness Nun behind my back"—which, in fact, they did—"but I'm not so sure you always will."

That spring morning in 1953, I was sitting at a café on Boulevard St. Germain, sipping my coffee and reading, with little interest, the oddly discreet reportage of the Baroness' death. It was not until I'd read the whole length of one column that my eye flicked up to the rather blurry photograph in the middle of the page. I knew the face at once. There was no thrilling, shocking sensation of *Could it be?* or *Surely it isn't!* There was only a moment of terrible and profound grief that I had discovered in this casual, ridiculous way that my long search was over. The image I had carried in my heart, in my mind, in the haunted heat of my loins, had been destroyed in a filthy hotel in the Paris slums. Two decades of memory ended there.

For it was soon after the death of her husband—although I didn't know he was the Baron Arvon—that I met Clara, ice-haired Clara, all ice except for the holocaust raging within her. We met by accident, or, to tell the truth, we didn't meet at all—I followed her. She appeared, as I later learned was the only way she could appear, as if from out of nowhere. I turned a street and there she was...only her back at first, but what an incredible back it was. She was made all of one line, one soft, curving line that rolled and swelled, spread and narrowed, moved from the curve of her shoulders to the small of her back and widened out to a stretch of hips that ran in a perfect curve around the slight swell of her buttocks, delicious globes that swayed ever-so-slightly beneath the grip of her all-white summer dress. The dress hung to the middle of her calves, but there the splendid line of her body reasserted itself in the shape of tanned flesh that blossomed out for a moment as if appealing

to a waiting hand and then tapered down to a chis-
eled ankle. Her hair was much longer than most
women wore theirs that year. What would she have
done with a mannish cut? She needed it just as it was,
lightly waved, softly rippling to her shoulders, incredibly casual despite the strangeness of its color—platinum-blue, like the color of a perfect diamond. Yes,
she was all ice like a diamond, but diamonds are born
of coal—and both burn.

For some minutes, I was so caught up in admiring
her back that I didn't think of increasing my pace.
Then, when I decided to catch up with her, she saved
me the trouble by turning a corner and sitting down
on the terrace of a café. It was a large terrace and
there was no one else on it, but I was too caught up
by the girl to make any pretenses. I sat down at the
table just beside hers.

It is difficult to describe a beautiful woman.
Most women you can describe are only pretty—
they have a flaw somewhere. But a beautiful
woman, one as beautiful as Clara was, can have no
feature better than the next; all features must coor-
dinate. Well, she sat at the next table, her face
expressionless, and she didn't seem to notice me.
She was tanned, but still her face was paler than
her calves, like a slightly darkened cream, and her
long eyelashes curved out black and fine from delicate lids above her eyes—those clear eyes, almost
the same color as her hair, which refused to notice
me. They stared straight out across the pavement
and were made arrogant by the way she kept her
chin raised. It was wonderful to see the graceful
sweep of that single line again leading from her
chin down the length of her straight neck and then
outward to form those breasts defying conceal-
ment, trying in every way to reveal themselves. I

could sense the warm elasticity of her nipples chafing at the cloth of her dress. I wanted to bend over to her and with no more ado than a "Mademoiselle, may I?" pluck the round softness from her bodice and bring a nipple to my lips.

When the waiter came, she ordered cognac, and so did I.

"On a day like this," I said to her as soon as the waiter had gone, "cognac is the wrong thing to have. It only makes you warmer."

"Is that so?" But she still wouldn't look at me.

"Well," I began, wishing I were a brilliant conversationalist, "well, yes, that's so. Alcohol increases the blood pressure...or something...and it makes the blood—well, you know. In any case, it makes you warmer."

"Then would you mind telling me why *you* ordered cognac?" She looked at me for the first time, her full lips gently parted.

I smiled, but she refused to smile back and merely continued to gaze at me distantly.

"Maybe," I told her, "I want to be warmer."

Not catching any but the most literal meaning of my statement, she spoke thoughtlessly: "And maybe I do too." She had hardly finished speaking before our conversation took on a new light in her mind and she could not prevent herself from smiling. Then she turned away from me and stared again at the pavement until the waiter brought our drinks.

"Would you mind if I joined you at your table?" I asked.

She sighed deeply, her magnificent breasts rising. "I would mind very much. In the first place, I am only very recently a widow. In the second place, even if I didn't think it improper to speak to a strange man, I must confess I have no inclination to."

"Why not?"

"I simply haven't. I find that most men labor under the delusion that they will soon be providing me with a pleasure I find altogether repugnant."

"*Most* men, you say. But that doesn't mean *all* men."

"Perhaps not. In all honesty, then, you are going to claim yourself one of the rare men interested in me only as a partner in aimless sociable conversation?"

I hesitated. "In all honesty, no."

"In that case, I think it best to bring our conversation to a close." And she sipped at her cognac.

"By the way, you said a minute ago that most men wanted to provide you with a pleasure you find repugnant. How can a pleasure be repugnant?"

She flushed and stared down at her drink. "I meant that it wasn't a pleasure—I meant that it was their pleasure, not mine. I meant—" She stopped abruptly and I realized she'd begun to cry.

I jumped from my chair and moved to her table.

"Look, I'm terribly sorry. I didn't mean to make you cry. Please forgive me."

"It's all right," she said, her voice calm but tears still coming into her eyes. "Just give me your handkerchief. Thank you."

"I'm really terribly sorry." Sitting down beside her I put my arm around her. My embrace was almost brotherly and she must have sensed this because, as her eyes slowly dried, I could feel that she was grateful for my comfort. It was this curious reversal in both of us—my fraternal affection and her gratitude—that made me understand it was not so much what I'd said that bothered her, but some deeper problem which, when evoked, could easily bring tears from her.

11

"If there's anything I can do for you," I said, "I'd like you to know you can count on me. You don't know anything about me, of course, but if you'll take my word for it, I'm a trustworthy person and—"

"There's nothing anyone can do," she shook her head. "It's all been done. It's finished. In the past."

I was silent because I knew she would say more. After a moment, she continued. "If only I could talk to someone. I see myself choking with my own misery in all the years ahead, saying nothing."

"You can talk to me. I'm a stranger to you, and I'm even a foreigner in your country."

"You're an American?"

"Yes."

She looked at me suddenly, her blue eyes searching across my face. "Could you meet me tonight?" she asked finally.

"Yes." .

"Be here, at this café, about midnight."

"I could pick you up somewhere else, if you'd like. I've got a car."

"No, that's impossible. Let's meet here."

She stood up and put a coin on the table.

"Goodbye," she said. "Until tonight." Her voice was husky and thrilling, and in my new role of father-confessor, I tried not to look at the voluptuous curves of her retreating form.

At a quarter of twelve, I was back at the same table. It was a heavy night, warm, damp, with a slice of moon standing like a crescent on the point of the church steeple in the square across the way. I had some misgivings about my rendezvous. Here was a hot, wet night, a night when moist flesh ought to be pressed up against other moist flesh. There was even a bit of moonlight to sift through a bedroom window

12

and glisten on undulating bodies caught in the raptures of love. But no; this was not for me. I had to be Mr. Good Samaritan, listen paternally to the problems of a miserable young woman. The only physical contact I could expect would be another fraternal embrace...if I were lucky. Maybe not even that. I oughtn't to bother waiting, I thought. But I waited.

By midnight, the café became a bit crowded with people taking a last cool drink after the theater or the movies. There was a great deal of noise, and I knew this wouldn't be the right place for a solemn talk. Then, suddenly, there she was, coming across the square as if she'd stepped right out of the darkness.

She was wearing a tight black dress now, and it was clamped against all her curves; as she walked, it hugged in against her loins and lay hungrily on the inside swell of her thigh. This dress was cut lower than the white one and, except for a long necklace of what appeared to be diamonds, her flesh swooped in an unbroken expanse halfway down the swell of her jiggling breasts.

It was going to be hard for her father-confessor; in fact, a part of me was already hard, and warmth tingled along my body. When she approached my table, everyone turned to stare.

"Let's get away from here," I said.

She nodded. I stood up, took her arm, and guided her to the corner in silence.

"Look," I told her, "we can go to another café, if you want. Or else we can just drive around the city. My car's down the street."

She hesitated. "I hope I haven't made a mistake."

"What do you mean?"

"Trusting you."

"You're so damn suspicious. You must think I'm

quite a man to be able to drive a car and get romantic with you at the same time."

She laughed. It was the first time I'd seen her laugh. It was a good throaty laugh, and I was dazzled by the even whiteness of her teeth and the sudden flicker of a pink pointed tongue.

"All right," she said. "We'll take a ride."

For five minutes we drove without exchanging a word. There was almost no traffic, and the breeze was wonderful as it fluttered through the window while we sped along.

"Do you want to begin?" I prodded.

"I'm trying to. It's so difficult when one has lived in silence for so long."

"So long?"

"More than four years. That's a long time. And I was such a talkative girl. My boyfriends used to say the only way to get me to shut up was to put—" She broke off.

"Go on."

"Yes, I must say it all. All, from the beginning. My boyfriends—" she took a deep breath—"used to say the only way to shut me up was to put a tongue or a penis in my mouth. That would keep me quiet all right. I loved things like that in those days. I loved to feel a man's warm body against me and to have his face rub against mine and then to feel dry lips moving over me, pushing to my mouth and then a sweet, wet tongue. I liked the other thing even better, taking a stiff organ in my mouth and coaxing at it, smothering it with the warmth of tongue and throat. My whole body would be pulling at it, calling its vital life to flow into my mouth. But I never did anything more—I mean, I didn't make love until I was married.

"I was raised in a town in the center of France. My

14

parents were fairly well-off, but they were very ambitious. If I had a rich boyfriend, I knew it was perfectly acceptable to bring him to my house at night and do whatever we wanted—and my parents knew about it. But if the boy was poor, and they found out I was seeing him, they'd call me a whore, a no-good. For me, a boy was a boy, it wasn't his money I liked in my mouth. When I was sixteen, a very rich man came to our town; he had come to spend a summer and it was great news. No one could talk of anything else all the time he was there—first they talked of his money, later of his eye for the girls, and last of all, of him and me. I didn't like him at all. He was almost fifty and had a terrific grey beard, an ugly scowl, and an enormous belly. Some of the girls in town slept with him and got money for it. I didn't sleep with him, though eventually I got all his money. One day, to everyone's astonishment, his big Rolls-Royce stopped in front of our house. My mother almost fainted with the pleasure of seeing the neighborhood come out to watch the fat man walk to our door. Without any explanation, he told my parents he would marry me. The fact was, that since he could not—as he had the other girls—rent me, he had decided to buy me. And, of course, no one ever asks a piece of goods if it wants to be bought; naturally, the owner is entitled to do what he wants with the article he owns. My parents received an excellent price for me. I haven't seen them since I left home, but I understand they are now the town's aristocracy, with a manor house and a half-dozen servants.

"At the end of the summer I went to Paris and lived with my fiancé's aunt while waiting for the wedding to take place. It was going to be a very elegant affair, and two months went into the preparation of it. I needn't tell you that Boris, my husband-to-be, wanted to anticipate, if not the union of our souls, certainly the union of our bodies. He was fairly champing at the bit to put his stiff thing between my legs. The way he looked at me! Fortunately, his aunt, a silly old lady who died the day after our wedding, had decided to act as my chaperone and never left the two of us alone in a room.

"Things were not too bad those two months before the wedding. I had everything a girl could want, and since I was only sixteen, the future, the wedding, the first physical acts with my hideous fiancé, seemed too far away to care about. And besides, the silly old aunt had a very handsome young butler who would sneak into my room at night and keep my mouth busy until morning. And he had a great deal to keep me busy with. His cock wasn't very thick, but it was exceedingly long. The head was like the cap of a mushroom on a thin stalk, and when swollen it took on a deep, dark hue. I enjoyed bringing it to that state and delighted in knowing that I could exercise such power over a young man. When I licked him he would be in a state of virtual ecstasy; his eyes would roll up in his head, his body would shudder, and his breath would come in small gasps. The nicest flush would spread across his chest and neck when I took the head in my mouth and sucked on it and he would raise his hips as if to urge me to draw more of him into my throat. I would oblige him, of course, but only after I'd licked the entire length of his shaft and massaged his balls with the tip of my tongue. By then he would be ready for me to accept him in my throat. I became quite proficient at milking his tool with my throat muscles, using them as I would later use my womanhood. And when he finally spurted in my mouth and bucked and jumped about from the excruciating sensations...well, the entire affair was heavenly. He even wanted me to run away with him, but I was too much of a fool to go."

We had both become so engrossed in what she was saying that neither of us noticed we had driven out of Paris into the suburbs. The hesitation with which she had begun her story now turned into a rather intense and distracted calm. She seemed to have forgotten about me and was instead reliving the episodes in her past. This made me feel odd, as if I were looking into somebody else's window, watching a strange man and woman go through the rite of love.

"Our wedding took place," she was saying, "at the end of November. I felt almost lost in the elegance of the affair, and yet I behaved superbly, for Boris' aunt had been giving me lessons. I knew the right amount of coolness or warmth to show everyone present. After the reception, we went to Boris' house. All the servants had been sent away. The place was silent, and for the first time I became tense with the expectation of what would take place. 'Come, my dear bride,' Boris said to me, 'I shall carry you to the sacrificial altar.'

"He picked me up, the great folds of my wedding gown billowing up around me. He carried me to the master bedroom. Tremendous candles burned all around the bridal chamber; heavy draperies hung across the windows and gleamed with the candlelight. There was something terrifying about the large bed. Boris was still carrying me. His arms tightened about my body and he said, 'When we go out into the world, Clara, you must remember that you are the aloof wife of a great man, that you are the mistress of many manors, that you are in the position to control almost everyone you meet. But when you enter this room you must forget all that, and remember only one thing—that you are my whore. You exist only for my pleasure. You are to be used as I see fit. Do you understand?' And his face bent close to mine.

"I said nothing, but looked away once more to the terrifying bed.

"'Do you understand?' he repeated, his arms squeezing me so tightly I could barely breathe. 'Do you understand?'

"I nodded. 'Then say it,' he commanded.

"'In this room,' I murmured quietly, 'I'm your whore. I exist only for your pleasure. I'll be used as you see fit.'

"He laughed as I spoke, and his beard slid across my face. Then, unexpectedly, his arms relaxed and flung me to the ground. I was too stunned to move, and even if I hadn't been, I don't think I would have dared to budge. Boris stood over me, an enormous monster. After a moment, he bent down with great effort and put his hands at the neck of my gown and pulled. I shrieked—more at the thought of the destruction of this expensive and beautiful dress than from any personal fear. He tore the dress down the length of my body, then pulled me to my feet and dragged the shredded cloth from my arms. His eyes widened and flamed to see me in my underthings. Reaching again, he ripped my brassiere from me, and my breasts trembled in their new freedom. He looked at them a long time before he put his finger out and slowly ran it across them.

"'Superb,' he said. 'Almost better than I expected.' His fingers moved to my nipples, and plucked at them delicately. I must admit there was something exciting in the sensation of his rough finger stroking them. Then he took them between thumb and forefinger and massaged them gently, then a little more fiercely, beginning to squeeze them, increasing the pressure gradually until pinpoints of flame-like pain licked into my breasts. He released me and his hands fell to my hips, to the elastic band of my panties. He rolled them slowly down my hips to the point below my navel. Lifting his finger again, he stroked the roundness of my belly, round and round, until involuntarily my body began to move with his finger, shimmying slightly round and round. Without warning, he once more grasped my panties, and with one violent gesture tore them from me and flung them across the room. His large hands were again on my hips; they moved downwards to my thighs, pulling my stockings as they moved. He bent and took my shoes and stockings off. I was completely naked, and he backed away from me and looked and looked, his eyes moving up and down. 'Excellent,' he whispered. 'Excellent. Now turn around.' I turned around and then back, and then around again; he made me go on turning, faster and faster, until my breasts rose out before me from my frenzied breathing and I became dizzy as I spun. 'Keep turning,' he said, and as I turned I saw him begin to remove his own clothing."

I could no longer go on driving. We were now out in the country and, since I couldn't concentrate on the dark roads, I pulled the car into a side lane and shut the motor. Clara didn't even notice. She was involved with her wedding night, half with terror at the recollection of what was coming, half with pleasure. She was breathing heavily. How I wished that I could then be looking at what Boris had seen, to see her spinning naked before me while I undressed. Hardly knowing what I was doing, I moved close to her and put my arm round her. She didn't seem to be aware of anything I did.

"I continued to spin," she said. "Each time I faced Boris I saw him tugging at his clothing or dropping an article on the floor. I was so dizzy I could hardly stand, but when I threatened to pause, he roared, 'Turn!' and I turned. He was naked to the waist and his chest seemed like a continuation of his thick beard—it was one thick mass of grey hair. Suddenly, he was all undressed except for his shorts. 'Stop turning,' he called. I stopped, but had to grab hold of a chair to keep from falling.

"'Now,' he said, 'get on your knees and crawl to me.' I did as he asked, and when I reached him he ordered me to pull his shorts down. I did, doing it slowly to please him, and when the garment had reached his loins his massive penis jumped out at me, almost touching my face. 'Did you ever see a bigger one than that?' he asked me.

"'No,' I told him. In fact I never had. Its length and width startled me; I could already feel it breaking me open, splitting me in half. When he had stepped out of his shorts he pushed the tip of his member against my lips, and slowly I opened my mouth. Its bulging head moved past my teeth and came to rest at the end of my tongue. The heat radiated into me, exciting me; I felt myself go damp and gluey in my womanhood, now twitching with the beginning of desire. He continued to push his penis into my mouth, slowly, slowly. But there was too much of it. I fondled the sac of his testicles, pushing my mouth closer to him, wanting to swallow his tool, but finding it too long for me. When there was room for no more, he roared, 'You will take it all into your mouth, as you will take it all into other parts of you. Relax, let it slip into your throat.' He continued to push it in; my throat and tongue ached with the burden of his stiff relentlessness. And somehow, at last, my face was smothered in his bush of hair, my chin resting against his scrotum. I was numb with this enormous invasion and felt its hot pulsing length throb against my tongue. He edged backwards, sliding it out of my mouth, then back again, down, down. His hands were on my head stroking me. I continued to lick him; in truth, there was very little else I could do. I was effectively his prisoner, though I didn't consider myself so at the time. I knew I would be made to pleasure him in any fashion he thought acceptable, and I was more than willing to do so despite my fear. I could barely fit my mouth around the girth of his enormous prick as I sucked it wildly. I dragged my tongue across the slit in the tip of his enormous cockhead and felt him shudder. Encouraged and eager to please, I swirled around the swollen knob and then swallowed him once again. I could feel him lodged deeply in my gullet and I struggled to draw breath at the same time. I teased his balls with my lips and ran my nose through the hair on his loins as he pistoned in and out of me.

"He grabbed hold of my shoulders and pulled me to my feet. 'You suck as if you spent your life with your face in a man's crotch,' he said. 'Now get on the bed; we'll see about your other openings.'

"I lay down and waited for him. He came to the foot of the bed and, since there was no footboard, but only two posts—one on either side of the wide bed—he leaned across and put a hand on each of my ankles. Pulling me toward him, he spread my legs wide, stretching them the width of the bed until each of my legs was held in place by putting my feet outside the bedposts. After the first agony of the wrench, I enjoyed the sensation. I felt my damp cunt thrust itself out freely. Boris stood above me looking between my legs. Then he knelt and drew his face down to my loins. His beard swept over my raw flesh, and then his thick lips were pressed against my vale of delight; his tongue shot out, and a shock of excitement tore through my body. The tongue lashed hotly in the meat of my crotch; it stopped at my clitoris and his teeth bit at it like blades. Then his tongue slid the length of my split, went down and under, back up again to the threshold of pleasure and darted in and out. I wanted to scream with delight; I only moaned. His hands rubbed fiercely across my body, gathered my breasts up like warm dough. He seemed to be drinking the juice of my loins, drowning in it, while his tongue explored my cavern."

It was driving me crazy to listen to her. Here, just beneath that black dress, lay those taut lips, squeezed together, hidden by thighs whose outline was clear to me. I could not prevent myself from pulling Clara closer to me. She continued to talk and she still seemed unconscious of me—unconscious of me, that is, as myself, but she was aware of that a man, some man, sat beside her, for her small hand moved from her side and came to rest upon my fly. I felt myself throbbing under her touch, and then suddenly one of her fingers slid into the space between the buttons and I felt the cool fire of her skin touch my flesh. I reached over and put my hand upon her knee, and her thighs gently moved apart. My fingers groped upwards under her dress, to the darkness, to the dampness. I groped slowly along her thighs, and all the time, she talked.

"He lifted his face from between my legs, his beard dripping with my juice. Sliding upward, he threw the whole weight of his body on top of me. I felt crushed by his enormity; I couldn't breathe; every inch of my body was carpeted by his flesh and hair. His wet beard kept rubbing over my mouth, and I was forced to taste the excitement of my own womanhood. His hands moved constantly—rubbing, stroking, squeezing, pinching. He grabbed my buttocks and squeezed until I shrieked, then his fingers slid between them and he stroked the tight, dry little opening. 'Later on,' he said, 'we'll make it larger. But now I want the wet one.' He took hold of my thighs and pushed until they were against my belly and my pussy was raised—hot pouting lips, waiting to be split apart. I saw his hand go round his penis. He guided it to the threshold of its home. I felt the magnificent heat pulse against me. The head edged slowly in, my thighs shot wide apart, and my legs went round in the air, kicking with impatience. The tip of his enormous cock sucked in and out of me gently, until I was so excited my fingernails tore at my husband's shoulders. 'In,' I cried, 'put it in. All the way in.' His mouth lapped across my breasts, then came to rest on my right nipple. He sucked hungrily, always moving his penis. 'Now,' he roared, and with one thrust I felt its length tear into me. Nothing existed but this wild painful lunge, and then it was lodged in me—that tremendous instrument. It beat like drums and affected every part of my body. I began to writhe hungrily, impaled on his lance, while Boris chewed at my nipples, bit at my breasts, pinched all over my body. The hot iron seemed to be inserted not only several inches into my loins, but everywhere—past my belly, into my chest, beside my heart. My heart matched its throbbing."

She had undone my buttons and her hand circled round my rod. She pulled tenderly. My fingers had come to the warm flesh of upper thigh and continued to move; I brushed over the soft hair—not at all surprised that she was not wearing panties. And then I was wild; I tore at her dripping rawness, my fingers pulling roughly. She moaned, and paused a moment in her story. Her eyes closed, head rolled backwards, hair like moonlight tumbling on the back of the seat.

Into the trembling moisture of her slit I dug my fingers. The hand that had been around her shoulders now slid into her bodice and circled a warm breast. Holding it tightly, I scooped it free. In the dimness I could see its pale perfect shape, its stiff dark tip. My face bent to it, my lips hungered at it, my tongue trembled across its spongy excitement. Then she went on talking again, and I wanted to shut her up. But she wouldn't. She was, I'm sure, in a sort of trance—and her excitement was four years old. She was hot with Boris' penis in her. I remembered what she'd said earlier—that the only way to shut her up was to keep her mouth busy. I lifted my head and our faces met powerfully; our tongues entwined, circling. After a moment, I broke away, and eased her head down until her lips kissed my pounding tool. She began to suck, abruptly, savagely, taking all of it into her mouth as if she wanted to swallow me along with it. My fingers were insane in her pussy. I wanted her to stop sucking so that I could fuck her, but it was impossible to pull her away. I was almost ready to explode; her soft lips and tongue manipulated my hard tenseness. Suddenly she stopped, sat up straight, and snapped her thighs together so that my hand was clamped in her; she continued her story.

"He lay on top of me for a moment, very still, as though he'd fallen asleep. Then suddenly he came to life and began tossing and thumping, lifting his weight from me and dropping it again. His penis thrust deep, moved out, was thrust again. It happened a thousand times, and each thrust seemed to wind me a little tighter. His thrusts became quicker, quicker, his cock grew larger and larger until we were scratching crazily at each other and I was bursting into pieces, and Boris' thick juice was pouring out of him, spilling into me like a fountain into the sky.

"We lay still for a little while, and then the horrible things began to happen. First I thought his bites were playful, but then the pain was too great to be pleasant. His teeth snapped at my neck and shoulders and breasts, digging into my flesh until blood flowed. I cried and tried to push him from me. 'Remember that you are my whore,' he hissed, and he slapped my face. He started to rise and pulled his diminishing tool from me; moving over me, he seated himself on my belly and began to beat me mercilessly. His hand slammed across my face; his huge buttocks jumped up and down on my stomach. All pleasure and excitement was beaten out of me. It must have gone on for half an hour, and when finally he had finished pounding me with his body, he started with shoes, then with a belt, and last of all he scraped the metal hook of a clothes-hanger across my flesh. I was limp and bloody, weak and faint. I wanted to die, and yet was terrified that Boris would kill me. His erection had returned more tremendous than ever; it terrified me and revolted me. 'Get on all fours,' he said. Every part of my body ached, but with the last resources of my strength I turned on my stomach and dragged myself into the required position. I felt him poking at my little hole. Then Boris climbed on top of me and without a moment's hesitation, drove his penis through my tight channel. I screamed and screamed; I could hear Boris sighing with a passion he had not known earlier in the evening. His arms went around me; one hand tore at my breasts, pulling them as he would a cow's udder, the other circled between my thighs. 'I like fucking your ass,' he moaned as he pounded into me and manipulated my clit with his hand. 'You like it too, don't you? Don't you?' I was unable to do anything but groan my agreement, for I feared what would happen if I didn't. I derived very little pleasure from the whole affair, even though Boris worked at my love-button like a madman. The pain radiating from my bottomhole was simply too intense, though Boris enjoyed himself immensely. The weight of him was almost unbearable as he drove his rod in and out of my orifice. All the while he commented about how my asshole seemed to suck at him, how the skin became distended as he drew back and puckered as he thrust forward. I could feel him swelling, swelling. His balls slapped my buttocks with each long, deep stroke. Even when he finally erupted, filling my anal canal with his hot cream, he wasn't done. His erection never diminished and he continued to drive his lance into my innards. He rode me like an animal. This intense agony continued almost until dawn.

Just before the sun came up, I went into a dead faint. When I awoke I was on the sofa; the blood-splattered bedsheets were on the floor. Boris himself lay like a monstrous mountain on the bare bed. His penis was again—or perhaps still—erect; it was repugnant to me. My body was a tortured wreck; I could move nothing but my head. And that was my life for four years. Boris' ingenuity never failed him; he had new and greater agonies at his beck and call. Sex became the horror of my life—the thought of it nauseated me, whether with him or any man. Many times I wanted to run away; even being a beggar would have been a better than that life. But it wasn't possible; he would have found me anywhere I went. And besides, I was watched all the time. He hired people to see I never strayed too far.

"During the day I played the part of the respected and cool wife of a great man. And my husband was the perfect gentleman in public. People often told me how surprised they were that my marriage was such a success; after all, they said, Boris was so much older than I. I smiled, knowing how rapidly they would change their minds if they could witness but one of our orgies.

"Not many months after our marriage I became pregnant. Boris was both delighted and infuriated. Delighted, because he had long dreamed of having a son and heir; infuriated, because his treatment of me had to become less brutal, both for the child's sake and because it would have looked very bad for him to have me visit my doctor with bruises, scars, and welts all over my body. It was then I decided that life would only be tolerable for me if I could keep myself pregnant as often as possible. When the child was born, and it was a girl, I was delighted. I thought Boris would surely want me to become pregnant again to try once more for a son.

"But I was mistaken. He despised the girl, and to my astonishment decided that I was too much of a fool to ever be able to bear him a male child. What's more, he was now unwilling to relinquish his more intense sexual pleasures for the minor pleasures of paternity.

"One morning, two or three months after little Angela was born, Boris came to my bedroom and said, 'Clara, my dear, a young man will visit you tonight.'

"'Who?' I asked.

"'You do not know him yet.'

"'I'm afraid I really don't feel up to meeting anyone new, Boris. Can't he be put off?'

"'I don't want any arguments.'

"I knew it would be safer for me not to argue, for although Boris never discussed our lovemaking during the day, he was apt to remember when I annoyed him, and would fiendishly take out his frustrations on me at night. 'Will he be coming for dinner or for coffee?' I asked.

"'For neither. You may expect him at eleven.'

"'At eleven? Isn't that a little late?'

"'Perhaps. Never mind. Go to bed whenever you like—but be sure,' he added fiercely, 'that it's before eleven. Do you understand? Be naked in your bed before eleven o'clock. Everything else will be taken care of. You may be certain of that.'

"Of course, I obeyed his instructions. I lay in bed wondering what new agony was in store for me. Where Boris was concerned, one never needed to be long at wondering. And so, soon after eleven, my bedroom door opened and a young man came into the room. He was very handsome and not much older than myself, but I no more desired him for a sexual partner than I did my husband.

"'You are the young man my husband told me to expect?' I asked, knowing that he was. But he barely looked at me; he said nothing. He walked to the foot of my bed and began to undress. When he was nude, he came around the side, his penis in his hand and, wordlessly, indicated that I was to manipulate it. I stroked it indifferently and passively allowed him to dart it into my mouth. He plunged it all the way down my throat so that his balls slapped my chin. And just as suddenly, he pulled back until just the swollen head was between my teeth. Then, rather impatiently, he flung me away from him and lay down on the bed, his red cock sticking into the air. The young man made signs for me to sit upon his instrument; I squatted over it while he squeezed my breasts and pinched my nipples, wriggling myself until his tip slid to my opening. As I was about to impale myself on it, he jerked his body, and his prick glided along my crack like a wheel in a track. I had to begin again, and again he jerked it away. Again I guided its head to my hole. This time he allowed me to drop down and the ramrod oozed deeply into me. At this point he moved his body, swinging his legs over the side of the bed and forcing me to lie down on top of him so that my legs, like his, hung down. His penis almost slipped out with our motions, and I forced myself down on it, screwing its hot length securely into me. He then reached across the bed, took the two pillows at its head and slid them under his hips so that I was lifted curiously with my behind in the air. It was then that I realized Boris had entered the room. He spread my buttocks and dug his fat limb into my bottom, then dropped over me so that I was sandwiched between the two men—a sandwich loaded with two enormous sausages, one thrusting me up, the other down. They fucked me without respite or remorse, one in my cunt and the other deep in my ass. I was their helpless pawn, to be manipulated as they saw fit, though for now they seemed to be content with filling me from both ends. It was truly an amazing sensation to feel those two large cocks inside me separated only by a thin membrane. They moved in opposite motions so that when one was plunging in the other was sliding out. The effect was of one unending, excruciating fuck. While they did this to me they squeezed and fondled my breasts, pinched my nipples, and kneaded my buttocks. I felt hands all over me, just as it seemed every inch of me was filled with those demanding cocks. They came simultaneously, releasing twin geysers of thick sperm into my pussy and ass. Their spasms seemed to go on interminably until their juices, and my own, began to dribble down my thighs and soak the bed.

"This young man—whose name I never learned—

became a regular visitor. Later Boris added a young woman to our orgies, and I was taught the pleasure—or horrors, depending on how you look at it, I suppose—of lesbianism. I don't know how many others joined us during my four years with Boris. There was a dwarf with a surprisingly enormous tool and for a while there was a tattooed man with a green penis and rose petals painted on his anus. 'Smell my flower,' he used to say. Now and then he would ask one of the other men to water the flower, and I would watch Boris or another go to it with delight.

"But none of these activities pleased Boris as much as the simple pleasure of torturing me. This he did only when we were alone, and rarely more than once a month. Once he said to me, 'When I have had enough of you, Clara, I will destroy you quite beautifully. I will fuck you until you are screaming with joy—and you know I can make you—and at the moment of your climax I will shove a sizzling hot iron up your ass. Do you think any woman could ask for a better death?'

"He was demented. It became very plain to me, though I was unable to effect an escape. My only pleasure lay in my daughter, Angela. Boris even threatened to make her join in our orgies. But I knew he never would, for no matter what infamies he sank to at night, his behavior was impeccable during the day. And I ultimately learned that to save his good name, he would forego even the pleasures of the flesh.

"Then, when we had been married nearly four years—"

She broke off suddenly, shuddered, looked at me and seemed for the first time in hours to remember who I was. Then she became aware of my hand still clamped between her thighs, and of her breasts hanging out of her dress.

"What are you doing to me?" she said. "Where are we?"

"We're in the country somewhere. And as for what I'm doing, I'm doing what you want."

"No, no, no." And she drove my hand away.

"This is no time to be coy," I said. "Less than half an hour ago you were sucking me savagely."

"That isn't true."

"No? Look here." In the pale darkness, blurs of her lipstick could be seen on my penis. "Let's go through with it now. The night's been leading to this."

"No! You're out of your mind. I'm through with filth, with men."

"Are you?" I forced myself against her, pushed my mouth to her tight, tense lips. At first they refused to part, but gradually, as my tongue flickered against them, they relaxed, softened, and finally spread for my kiss. My hand went once more to her thighs, and once more my fingers caressed her wet slit and her mound. When we broke apart passion seemed to make her eyes glow. We undressed hurriedly, left the car, and walked into the meadow beside the road. The first tremor of dawn showed in the sky as I turned to look at Clara and saw all that Boris had seen. Almost all. But as we tumbled into the grass I saw the rest, parting gently, smiling pinkly, empty and lonely and waiting to be filled with the tongue that jutted from my loins. I gently licked her nipples as I moved between her thighs. My hands seemed to have a life of their own, touching prodding, separating, caressing. My cock seemed impossibly hard as she took it in her hand and stroked it, then guided it to the gleaming beacon of her slit. I lowered myself to her and made contact with her moist warmth. I felt a luxurious thrill as I sank into her, stopping only when my belly came to rest on hers. She sighed as I began kissing her neck, her shoulders, the swell of her breasts. My hips moved slowly, drawing my hot shaft in and out. Her sugar walls gripped me tightly and imbued my aching tool with a sensitivity of which I didn't think it capable. She raised her hips up to meet my thrusts and matched my every movement. She was magnificent...and I was her devoted servant immediately. My sole thought was to give her pleasure. I rotated my hips and exulted in her smiled response and the increased pressure of her legs around my back. She seemed to draw me into her even more deeply; I began to thrust harder and faster. Her breath came in short, ragged gasps. I pumped with short, quick strokes. My cock was ready to explode; it had swollen until it could no longer contain the tide of our passion. My sperm erupted into her in a steady stream as she cried out her own rapture. When we were finished we lay still, overcome by the intensity of the orgasms and our emotions.

We were lovers for only three months. We always met after midnight and drove out to the location of our first lovemaking. Our coupling was always violent, and each of us was insatiable. We could neither of us have enough. But we would have to leave off before the sun rose.

"I've got to get home," she'd say. "It wouldn't do for Angela to know I've been out. It's difficult enough to keep the servants from missing me, although I've changed all their rooms around so that it's practically impossible for them to know I've gone. I don't want them gossiping—the child might hear it."

It was always Angela. I grew jealous of her invisible presence. It was because of her I couldn't come to

Clara's house. It was because of her that Clara refused to meet me during the day.

"I want her to know she can depend on me every moment of the day," Clara told me. "She must always know where I am. She must trust me completely."

"Hadn't you left her the day we met?"

"That was an exception. It had to do with Boris' will. I've told you he wasn't French. On that particular day I had to see the ambassador. In fact, darling, if we hadn't met at that time, we probably never would have met."

"We were fated to meet."

"Yes," she sighed, "we were."

These were always tender conversations following our passion, while we lay against each other in the dewy meadow. When the nights became cooler we had to seek out barns, and night after night I pumped away at Clara while cows watched us curiously. Finally, I asked her to marry me.

"Impossible."

"Why?"

"Because of—"

"Angela." I finished the sentence for her.

"Yes."

"Angela. Angela. You should get *her* to fuck you—then you wouldn't need anyone else at all."

Clara laughed. "She wouldn't be as good at it as you."

"Look, Clara, we can't go on like this, hiding in meadows and barns, meeting only at crazy hours. I want you for more than just a few fleeting moments.

"And don't you think I want the same thing? But we have to go on like this."

"What do you mean—go on? How long? All our lives?"

"Our lives aren't that long. Think of being lovers just as we are for another twenty years."

"It won't be fun in the winters."

"We'll think of something."

But we never thought of anything. Or, that is, I was full of ideas, but *she* wasn't having any of it.

"But Angela—" she'd say.

During our last two weeks together we spent more time fighting than making love.

"Something's got to be figured out or—" I began.

She interrupted me. "Or what?"

"Or we'll have to stop seeing each other."

"No!"

I could see she was frightened. "I'm serious, Clara."

"I'll go crazy if you leave me."

Now and then I'd try to take her home or, after leaving her at dawn at the café where we met at midnight, I'd try to follow her. It was impossible. She'd change taxis three or four times.

Throughout the last week, we didn't sleep together. I'd meet her at the cafe, ask her if she'd changed her mind.

"No," she'd sob through her tears. "Can't we go on like this?"

I'd walk away, get in my car and drive around the city, returning late at night, after the café had closed, though Clara was long gone.

The last night I was sure she was going to change her mind. But she didn't.

"You don't know what will become of me," she said.

"You'll be all right," I said. "You'll have to be all right for Angela."

I left without looking back. She wasn't there the next night, or the next. For a month I went to that café every night, then out to the freezing autumn meadows, then to the barns where the cows had witnessed our lovemaking.

34

There was no way to find her. I didn't know any name for her but Clara, and when I hired a detective I was amazed to learn there were hundreds of women in Paris with silver-blue hair. I knew it was useless, and I knew then that the mistake had been mine—that Clara in the barns and meadows was better than no Clara at all. I stayed in Paris, waiting at the café for that summer day—and Clara—to return. She was never there.

Since that time, except for the war years, I've come back to Paris every year or so, and I always try to extend my visit until after the day on which we'd met. But she seemed to have vanished completely; not until that spring day in 1953 did I hear of her again. We might have gone on, as she had reasoned, for twenty years. How quickly those twenty years have passed; how empty they've been; how full they might have been.

I was now a man in his middle years whose chase was over. Or was it? Perhaps now, knowing who she was, I could find out what the last twenty years of her life had held for her.

I waited a day or two, watching the papers for more news of Clara's death. There was nothing. The story of her death vanished, much as she had vanished.

Three days after the story appeared, I noticed a small item in the obituary column of one newspaper. It merely said that the Baroness Arvon was to buried that day at the family's private burial grounds, and that she was mourned by her only daughter.

Early the next morning I phoned Angela Arvon.

CHAPTER TWO

II.

The address was unlisted, but I found the phone number in the directory. It was still listed under the name of Baron Boris Arvon.

On the second ring, a man answered.

"May I speak with—" I hesitated, not knowing exactly what title the girl laid claim to. Finally, I said, "May I speak with Mademoiselle Arvon?"

"Who is calling, please?"

It was only then I realized how futile my effort was. What would my name mean to a girl so freshly bereaved of her mother? The name would mean nothing; she would refuse to speak to me.

"Howard Cunningham," I said. I had never spoken my name so hopelessly.

"Will you hold on a moment please, sir? I'll see if Mademoiselle is at home."

Doubtless she won't be, I thought. But then, to my surprise, I heard a woman's voice speaking to me.

"Mr. Cunningham?"

"Yes."

"This is Angela Arvon. Are you the American Mr. Cunningham, an old friend of my mother?" Her voice was much softer than her mother's had been. Clara's voice had been husky, sensual.

"Yes," I replied. "I'm surprised you know about me."

"I don't know about you—or very little, in any case. Do you think you could come over here, even for a very few moments?"

"Indeed I could."

"Can you come now, this morning?"

"Yes," I said, and she gave me the address.

The Arvon mansion lay in the Bois de Boulogne. It was an enormous house, rather ugly on the outside except for the formal gardens already in bloom and the depth of the chestnut trees that bounded three sides of the estate.

I drove up to the house, through the high gates, and up the driveway. I parked several yards from the terrace where the Arvon chauffeur took over and drove my car around to the back of the house. As I climbed the steps to the door, I found myself trembling. The aura of Clara was everywhere; I could feel her in everything around me.

Even in the girl who opened the door. She was the age her mother had been when I had known her, but she was paler than Clara. Her hair was cut like her mother's, but was a different color—rich, soft auburn. And her eyes were green. She was in deep mourning, and her smile was a little mournful as well as she asked me to come into the house. Walking ahead of me, Angela showed me to the salon, and it was only when she was at a slight distance from me that I saw how much shorter she was than Clara.

"Please sit down, Mr. Cunningham. What do you drink this time of day?"

"Anything at all."

She poured two sherries, then sat down beside me on the sofa. I was trying hard not to look at her.

"Your mother spoke of me?" I asked.

"Not until the day before her death. And she didn't say very much about you."

"Would you tell me what—"

"She said, 'Angela, I think an American named Howard Cunningham will phone here during the next few days. I want you to give him this envelope.' I asked her why she couldn't give it to you herself, and she smiled. 'I may not be able to see him. Please don't question me, darling, just do as I say. And be nice to him—because I loved him very deeply.' That was all she told me. Wait, I'll get the envelope for you."

She stood up, crossed the room, and returned, handing me the letter.

"If you would like to read it now, please go ahead. I'll leave you alone for a few minutes."

I tore the envelope open and found two sheets of paper inside; each bore the Arvon crest. The first sheet was dated the day before her death, and it read:

My dearest Howard—

I have waited almost twenty years to write this to you. Now at last I have come to do it, but I have so little time that I must hurry. I I love you. I have never stopped loving you. And I want you to know everything that has happened to me because you failed me when I needed you so terribly. I told you I would go crazy. I have, but it is a calculated madness that takes hold of me between midnight and dawn—our hours. I enclose a list of people whom I want you to see. It is an incomplete list of my madness, but it is composed of people who should remember your name. Most of them have seen you, as I have seen you—as I drove slowly by our café on the anniversaries of our meeting. I saw you, in fact, last summer. You've aged, of course, but I think you are handsomer, riper-looking. How much I yearn for one more night with you in the meadow.

Go to see the people listed; but go to see them only in the order in which they are listed.

I think most of them will tell you what you want to know.

My death has brought you to reading this. Along with this note I am leaving one to Angela which she will find the day after my death. She will pay a great deal of money and the newspapers will write nothing more of my death. It would not even be written about the first time—but it must—so that you will know, so that you will come to my house, Boris' house. When you've seen all the people I've listed, I want you to come back once more to this house.

I've never stopped loving you.

—Clara

The second sheet of paper had six names and addresses on it. I stared at the names blindly, remembering Clara, sipping sherry.

Angela came back into the room and sat down beside me.

"I'm so glad you're here, Mr. Cunningham. We were the only people she loved."

"Yes," I sighed. "I hope you didn't fail her as badly as I did."

"I've always been aware how much she gave up for me. And I've tried to make her sacrifices mean something. But you—would you tell me when you knew my mother?"

41

"Not long after your father died. We broke up because I wanted to marry her. She wouldn't, because..." My voice trailed away.

"Because of me."

We were silent then and I watched her breathing heavily beside me.

"I'd better go," I said. "There are some people your mother wanted me to see for her."

"Will you come back again? Please do."

"Thank you. I'd like to very much. When I've seen these people."

We stood up and she gave me her hand. I couldn't resist drawing her toward me and kissing her on the forehead; it was a paternal contact, much like my first with her mother. But as my lips touched her cool skin she seemed to press herself against me. I didn't want to relinquish our closeness, but at last I broke away. Angela's cheeks now had a darker color than they'd had a moment before, and her green eyes glistened. I stroked her face gently.

"You're so much like your mother."

She put her hand over mine and drew close to me again.

"I have to go," I murmured.

"Yes...." But neither of us moved.

I felt the freshness of her youth against me, and for all my efforts at control I knew my excitement was bulging against my trousers. Her belly pressed against the bulge and she shuddered as if having been in contact with a flame.

Looking down, I could see into the neck of her dress. Her breathing was heavy and I saw the pale mounds of her breasts rise and fall. They curved gently from the center of her chest and seemed to sway to the sides. She made a deliberate gesture and two pink tips flickered for a moment, then were hidden. I knew that if I didn't move there might be regrettable incidents.

"I'd better go," I said and stepped away from her.

"I'll have your car brought around front." Her eyes looked down to the bulge at my fly, then she brushed past me and went out of the room.

"It'll be ready in a moment," she said when she came back. I followed her out of the salon, through the central hall to the door of the house. As if by accident, she moved until she was directly before me and brushed against my loins. Through my trousers and through her mourning clothes, I felt the roundness of her buttocks. She moved sideways, subtly, cat-like.

Then the car was there.

"Here you are," said Angela, turning to face me. We shook hands. "I look forward to seeing you again."

She watched me get into the car and drive to the gates of the estate. How *much* like her mother she is, I thought.

CHAPTER THREE

III.

Of the six addresses Clara had left for me, the first two were in Paris, the third was on the Riviera, the next two were in Paris, and the last was somewhere near the Pyrenees. It would have been easier to see the third and sixth consecutively, rather than return to Paris in between, but Clara must have had her reasons for insisting upon the order. Besides, I had gone on so many trips because of her, one more would not cause me any great discomfort.

The same day I met Angela Arvon, I telephoned the first person on the list, a man named Peter van Drooft. A woman answered the phone.

"May I speak with Monsieur van Drooft, please?"

"He's busy just now. Could I have him call you back?"

"No, I'm not going to be at my hotel all day."

"Could you call back in, say, thirty minutes?"

"Yes, all right."

I called back, but he was still busy. When I

phoned a third time the woman asked me if I was ringing for an appointment. I told her yes.

"He'll be able to take you at four o'clock today," she said.

"That's fine." I hung up wondering if he were a doctor.

I arrived at the apartment house fifteen minutes early. It was an old, rather shaky-looking building, and since there was no concierge, I had to strike matches to read the list of tenants on the wall at the front of the stairs. Van Drooft was on the fifth floor.

It was a great effort to walk the steps because the staircase was narrow and each step very high. I was breathing heavily when I reached the fifth, and last, story. There were two doors on the landing, one of which had no knob. I knocked at the other.

"Come in," said a woman's voice. It was the voice I had spoken to on the telephone.

I turned the knob and entered a small anteroom. Aside from the desk at which the woman sat, there were only three pieces of furniture—two wooden chairs and an ash-stand between them.

"Are you Mr. Cunningham?"

"That's right."

"Would you sit down? Mr. van Drooft will see you in a moment."

She was about forty and very fat. Her too-black hair was fixed in a thousand little curls, like springs, that trembled when she spoke. Her round white face was thickly powdered, and two bright spots of red glowed on her cheeks. She wore too much lip-stick, too much mascara over her enormous black eyes, too much blue eye shadow, and her eyebrows had been shaved and painted over with a thin black line, like a moustache.

The lace neck of her dress was cut low over the squeezed line of her breasts. The breasts themselves made me think that two watermelons had been shoved into her bodice.

She caught me staring at her and she smiled, her thick red mouth splitting open on little yellow teeth.

Suddenly a man's voice shouted through the door behind my chair, "Colette!"

Colette stood up, turned around and moved a little knob in the wall behind her desk. She looked into it. The man's voice mumbled something and Colette said, "All right." She shut the knob, rubbed her hands on her hips and walked to the door behind me.

"Excuse me," she said.

At the moment she opened the door, something insisted I turn. I did in time to see a barren-looking room and two naked young men, one of whom was bent over, hands on knees. The other stood behind him, his penis in a state of half-erection. The door closed.

Curiosity getting the better of me, I left my chair and went to Colette's desk, then quickly turned the knob in the wall. Once it was open I could see into the next room. It was clearly a photographer's studio. I couldn't see the photographer himself, but I could see the two young men. They were now both standing up. Colette waddled into my line of vision and I saw her make a great effort and tug her dress over her head. She was naked underneath; roll after roll of loose flesh enfolded her body, and as she moved, all the folds trembled and danced. The small triangle of brown pubic hair was almost hidden by the doughy thighs that leaned over it. Her enormous breasts hung down heavily, ending in purplish nipples. She wore nothing but blue suede shoes. She lifted herself onto a white table and spread her thighs as wide as she could. Her pussy was a pink gash barely visible in the fleshy folds. The two boys approached her. One of them, the dark one, had an erection, but the blond one was pulling his rod hurriedly, trying to get it hard.

"What's the matter?" said the voice that had called Colette from behind the door, but whose owner I couldn't see. "Can't you get it up?"

"I'd like to see you get it up if you had to fuck this old wreck," said the blond boy.

Colette laughed. "You ought to see him get it up, kid. Isn't that right, Peter?" Then she lifted her arm and took the boy's tool in her fat hand. She pumped it expertly up and down and ran her thick palm over the head. It began to swell in her fist as the boy fondled her tits. When it was erect, she said, "Better shove it in fast, honey—before it goes down."

She leaned back and the boy wedged himself between her thighs. In an instant his cock was lost in Colette's mountain of soft flesh. He shoved it well in and thrust once or twice. The other young man got behind the first and inserted the tip of his penis into his friend's anus.

"Hold it now," said the photographer. They held it.

There were a few clicks and some brushing sounds. Then they changed positions—one boy in front, and one behind Colette. Next there were some close-ups: Colette smiling broadly with a penis in each ear; Colette smiling broadly with a penis in her mouth and one between her breasts; Colette's pussy smiling broadly as one of the young men lapped at it.

"That's all," said the photographer. "You boys get dressed in the other room."

I snapped the knob back over the opening and returned to my chair. I was hardly seated when the

49

door opened behind me and Colette, thrust respectably back into her dress, entered the room.

"Mr. van Drooft will see you now," she said.

She closed the door behind me as I passed into the studio. Van Drooft was fussing with a lens. He was about my age, I surmised, but because he was very thin he seemed a bit older. His smile was friendly.

"Mr. Cunningham?" he asked.

I nodded.

"What can I do for you, sir?"

"I've come at the request of—" I was about to say "Baroness Arvon," but then decided that it was unlikely she had told him who she was. "Clara. She had sort of platinum-blue hair. I don't know."

"Clara," he repeated with some amazement. "What a long time it's been since I saw her."

"She's dead," I told him flatly.

"Ah, that's too bad."

"Yes. She left a letter for me asking me to see you. She said you would tell me things."

"Cunningham, Cunningham," he said very quietly. "You must be Howard Cunningham."

"That's right."

"Good heavens, I never thought you would actually show up. I have a package for you. I've had it ready for almost twenty years. It'll take me a while to dig it out. But first I suppose we ought to talk. Are you free now?"

"Yes."

"Well, I have no more appointments today. Why don't you come into my living room and I'll tell you anything you'd like to know about Clara."

I followed him into the next room where the two boys were still dressing. Van Drooft showed me to a chair, then poured two glasses of wine and sat down opposite me.

"Why don't you hurry up?" he said to the young men.

"We're hurrying," they answered. We were all silent until they buttoned themselves up and went out through the studio.

"To our memory of Clara," van Drooft toasted, and sipped his wine. "Now what can I tell you?"

"Everything."

"Ah, but everything is too much."

"No, I'd like to know everything."

"To the last detail?"

"To the last detail."

"Then I begin on an autumn night many years ago. I was a very young man, a photographic artist. For me, the camera was like tubes of paint. I didn't want to be a businessman; I wanted to make pictures that would be art. At that particular time, I was most interested in faces. I was always looking for an interesting face. When I saw Clara the first time, I thought—here is an interesting face, a face that suffers. And, I must confess, I also thought it was a beautiful face.

I saw her on the terrace of a café one cool autumn night so many years ago. I was only passing by, but the instant I saw that desperate face I stopped and sat down at the table next to hers. I wondered how I could dare ask a woman so obviously unhappy to come pose for me. I was still thinking of an approach when suddenly a very abrupt young man came charging up the pavement. This, I take it, was you. Naturally, I overheard their conversation; even had I not been sitting so close to Clara, I would have heard it, for this foolish young man—yes, Mr. Cunningham, he was a foolish young man—shouted and ranted. He said, 'Clara, I've come for the last time. Have you changed your

51

mind?' The girl said nothing. He repeated, 'Have you changed your mind?'

"And she said, 'How can I? You know it's impossible.'

"'It isn't impossible. You'll have to do as I ask—or we're through.'

"'No, please. I beg you not to say that.'

"'It's true. We're finished. I won't come back again.'

"'You don't know what will become of me,' she said.

"He replied, rather nastily, I later realized, 'You'll be all right. You'll have to be all right for Angela.'

"Then the young man turned and disappeared. The girl wept silently. At that point, I decided to leave, but then, in spite of myself, I spoke to her. You think it was selfish of me? Perhaps, but I was an inconsiderate young man. And although generally I was rather timid, where my art was concerned I was headstrong. So I said, 'I couldn't help overhearing your conversation. Is there anything I can do for you?'

"She didn't seem to hear, so I repeated the question.

"'No no no,' she said through her tears.

"I realized it would be useless to insist, so I took a piece of paper from my pocket and wrote on it:

I'm a photographer and I should like to do some studies of your face. I'm not in a position to pay for such services but you will have copies of the pictures in payment. If you feel you might be generous enough to spare a few moments to me one day, I'll be very grateful.

I wrote my name and address, put the note on her table and left the café.

"I heard nothing from her for a week or ten days. Then, late one night, as I was reading in bed, there was a knock at the door. I put my trousers and robe on over my pajamas, went through the studio and anteroom, and opened the door.

"'Mr. van Drooft,' Clara said, handing me the note I had left at the café.

"I pushed the note aside, and said, 'As if I would have forgotten you. Please come in.' She followed me into the room where we are seated now. 'This is certainly a strange time to accept my offer.'

"'I'm sorry, but it's the only time I have.'

"I took her coat and she sat down. My eye—both as a man and photographer—drank in the body that her dress did little to conceal. We talked only a little that evening because we were soon involved in photography. She was a very patient model and enjoyed the work immensely. Once or twice I apologized for not being able to pay her, and finally she said, 'I don't need the money, and I'm perfectly delighted that my being here is of any use to you.'

"We continued working, with only occasional pauses, for three or four hours. During our breaks, we drank wine and coffee, and spoke a little, but the conversation was extremely impersonal. Frankly, I didn't want her to feel that I had lured her up to my place on false grounds, and so I myself never brought the talk around to ourselves. She, on the other hand, may have taken my conversation for a sign of coldness, and consequently wouldn't talk of herself. This happened not only that first night but during the many nights thereafter, because, Mr. Cunningham, Clara began to come very frequently to my studio.

"After a couple of weeks doing only studies of her face, I began to take full portraits of her with different costumes and different arrangements. She went into this with a great deal of enthusiasm and even began bringing wonderful costumes along with her. The first time I wanted to photograph her in costume I was rather embarrassed about it, so I asked if she'd mind putting the dress on.

"'I'd love to,' she said.

"'You can change in the salon,' I told her.

"She smiled rather strangely and said, 'As you wish,' and went into the unlighted salon leaving the door open behind her. I was arranging the studio for the next shot and the rustle of her clothing disconcerted me. Looking up once, I saw her standing naked in the shadows of the other room. I turned away quickly, but the suggestion of her flesh burned into me. It was the same way every time she changed in or out of costume—there would always be that one single opportunity to see her flesh in the darkness. Once, perhaps unconsciously, I left the light on in the salon. She said nothing about it, but she took longer making her changes, and I looked at her lengthily that time, watching her casual motions. After that I always left the light on: and eventually she began to dress more or less in the doorway between the two rooms. As it finally happened, she never left the studio at all when the change had to be made. And when she changed, I ceased to bother with the arrangements in the studio, but watched her instead. She would move with impossible slowness: each button, each hook, would take minutes to undo. She would lower her dress gracefully, each inch of her body coming into the light like a revelation. Stepping out of the dress, she would stretch herself as if free at last, and then begin the long process of loosing her brassiere. Her breasts would emerge and the nipples stare at me like eyes asking, *Why don't you come closer?* Every part of that body was firm, yet soft. I wanted to photograph it, and at the same time I wanted to possess it.

"Once when she was completely nude, she turned full upon me, and said, 'Peter, wouldn't you like to photograph me like this?'

"'I'd love to,' I replied and began to arrange the composition. She was very passive for these pictures and I had to touch her to get her into the right attitudes. It was an effort to keep calm when my hands circled her arm or her shoulder or the smooth warmth of her legs. She smiled, saying nothing, occasionally asking, 'Is that better?' At times, relaxing after a picture, her thighs would move inadvertently apart and I'd glimpse the inviting line that divided her fur. I'd expect the thighs to separate even further, and they would—but only slightly, enough to hint that a feast lay between them. My breath growing short, heavy, I'd stare frankly down, and suddenly the thighs would close like a trap.

"The nude photographs went on for a week or ten days, and then one evening when Clara arrived, she said, 'Peter, I've been reading the most interesting article—all about color film. Have you ever tried using any?'

"'Good heavens, no. Do you know how expensive that stuff is? I couldn't possibly afford it.'

"'I thought you'd say that, so do you know what I've done? I've ordered a great deal of it. I thought it might be fun to try out.'

"'I won't be able to accept it, Clara. I could not pay you for it and I can't accept a gift—'

"'Oh, nonsense, Peter. You're so stodgy. It must be all your cold northern blood.'

'Only my father was northern. My mother was Spanish.'

"She laughed tauntingly. 'Who'd ever have guessed it? Do you mean to say that somewhere within you is a big, long, hard passionate streak?'

"Since this big, long, hard passionate streak had been violently evident at least twice every night for the past two months, I refused to comment on it. I could not explain my behavior then, nor can I now, except under the vague and rather hypocritical-sounding word: honor. I had asked Clara to come to me as a model, and although a change in our relationship was what I wanted more than anything else—and, clearly, Clara was not against it—possibly the time was not yet ripe. If the Spaniard in me longed to throw himself on top of this ravishing woman, the Dutchman's iron voice whispered restraint. The Dutchman seemed to be in control at present, but the Spaniard was driving himself and his alter-ego crazy.

"But to return to our conversation, I said, 'I'm sorry, Clara, I don't think I ought to accept.'

"'Peter, honestly, you've given me so much pleasure in this studio—and I'm certain you'll give me lots more—that I'd like nothing better than to offer you a little something in return. Won't you accept?'

"She was undressing as she spoke, and when she was altogether naked, she came close to me, and said, "Won't you accept?'

"'I shouldn't,' I replied.

"'But you will…'

"My hand twitched with desire. 'Yes, I will.'

She moved until our bodies were touching, her breasts jutting against the front of my shirt. She filled my eyes, my senses. I wanted nothing more than to tear my clothes off and penetrate every orifice of her body. Abruptly, I turned away. I walked into the salon, poured myself a drink, and then another.

When I returned to the studio, I was calmer, and Clara lay on the sofa. She smiled and said, 'I'm very happy you've accepted my offer.'

"'The only thing is, of course,' I told her, 'that I don't know the first thing about color equipment. I don't have the lighting and—'

"'Oh, that's all right. I've taken care of everything.'

"And indeed she had. For, one afternoon, about a week later, two men came to my studio with a tremendous crate. Clara had seen to everything—film, lighting, developing, a camera, and there was even a small chest of makeup for color photographs. The rest of that afternoon, and all through the evening, I read the books and manuals that had come with the parcel. By the time Clara arrived that night my head was whirling with all I'd learned.

"'I've spent the past eight hours,' I said to her, 'trying to get some idea how to work all this.'

"'Did it come today?' she asked with some disappointment in her voice. 'I didn't think they'd deliver it until tomorrow.'

"'It doesn't matter, does it?'

"'N-no, of course it doesn't matter. But let's not begin until tomorrow.'

"'That's fine with me,' I said. 'I was going to ask if we couldn't wait because, frankly, I'm exhausted. Would you like to go out for a bit? I'd like some air.'

"Outside, the night was cold and, since it was so late, there was no one on the street. We walked for a while along the Boulevard Montparnasse and then I suggested we stop in at one of the cafés. I knew a great many people who frequented these cafés and most of them had begun wondering why I no longer appeared in the evenings. My suddenly appearing with one of the most ravishing beauties anyone had ever seen would give them a turn.

"But Clara refused.

"'I'd rather not,' she said. 'I don't want to be seen. It's not likely, but there may be people I know.'

"'Are you ashamed to be seen with me?' I was fairly angry, particularly since I'd just been thinking how proud I'd be to be seen with her.

"'No, it has nothing to do with you, Peter. Normally I'd be proud to be seen with as talented a man as you. But, well—look, let's go to a small place down one of the side streets and I'll try to explain.'

"'All right,' I said, rather sullenly.

"That was the first night Clara ever talked about herself. Her story was vague and broad. How much of it was true, I still don't know. In any case, she told me of her daughter and how she didn't want the child to know of her absences. It was also that night that she spoke of you, Mr. Cunningham, and made the request that all the photographs—or, rather, copies of them—be made into a package and saved for you.

"'How will he know about me if you don't intend to see him again and don't know his address?' I asked.

"'He'll know. I promise you. It may be a good many years, Peter, but one day he'll come to your studio.'

"I have that package for you—and there are, indeed, some extraordinary pictures among them. Well, that night, Clara and I spoke a good deal—mostly about ourselves. This turned out to be delightful since it did, in a way, begin the change in our relationship. We grew closer that night, just by talking until dawn. And suddenly the sun came up, and Clara became panicky. I found a cab for her and she pecked me on the cheek and started to climb into the car.

"'I'm so glad,' she said as I was shutting the door after her, 'that you're prepared to accept what I offer.'

"She was smiling when the taxi rolled down the street.

"The following night she was strange from the moment she entered, and there was a rather mocking expression on her face. She said very little and we decided to begin with the color film at once.

"'I'd better put the makeup on,' she said and opened the chest that had come with the other equipment.

"She undressed then, taking even more time at it than was usual for her, and she was more orderly than usual. When she stepped out of her dress, she left it lying on the floor. Her brassiere dropped on top of it and her hands rubbed underneath her breasts, raising them so the pink roses at their tip reached toward me.

"'We'll have to put some makeup here,' she said, indicating her nipples, "so they'll show up better in the color. Will you help me do it?'

"I nodded, but found it impossible to say a word. Then slowly, she began to roll her panties down her hips, down her thighs, down her legs. The triangle of her groin seemed somehow new to me, as if I were seeing it for the first time. It was the Spaniard in me, I suppose, whose eyes I could no longer resist using. He, I, we, saw the body that must be taken, taken violently, and in every conceivable way. I wanted to use every part of her, for every part seemed ready, pulsing, thumping, singing with anticipation.

"Her panties were on the floor, and with the point of her foot she kicked them to the little pile of clothing.

"'First I think you ought to powder me,' she said.

"I went to the makeup chest and took the soft

powder puff out of its wrapper, then broke the lid off the powder box and dipped the puff into it until it was rich with the stuff. Approaching Clara, I began to pat her shoulders gently with the pink dust: its perfume rose around us. She turned and I patted the powder down her back and to the tops of her buttocks—there, I hesitated.

"'You'd better do it lower down, too. Don't you think so?'

"I obeyed her, the puff moving across the roundness of her flesh. My fingers tingled at the contact. Beginning to powder her thighs, they moved apart gently, but slightly, so that only a few fine feathers of the puff could edge between. Abruptly she swung around and, since I was kneeling, my face was against another powder puff, her own. I backed away and lifted myself to my feet, not looking into her eyes, and I started powdering her neck, then her chest. I circled the feathers around her breasts and she sighed. My fingers trailed back and forth across her nipples. Kneeling once more, I powdered her belly and the breadth of her hips, and let the puff run over the triangle of pale hair.

"'No, not there,' she said. 'A darker color for the hair would be better.'

"'Later,' I said, unwilling to stop.

"I patted the front of her thighs and again they moved open, but this time wider than I'd expected, wide enough to see the moisture glued to her hidden moss. I powdered the inside of her thighs, arching my hand so that my knuckles slid between the wooly lips. She shuddered and groaned. My heart was wild with passion, and I was about to thrust my mouth into her warmth when her thighs clamped together.

"'My knees,' she said. 'You're forgetting my knees.'

"I powdered her knees and calves quickly for my interest was concentrated above. Drawing away, Clara said, 'Some rouge on my nipples.' But, since I didn't move, she walked to the chest and brought the rouge to me. Standing up, I began to apply the color to her engorged tips, stroking and patting, then working the color with my fingers. I took some more rouge and put a few pale streaks on her lush breasts to heighten their tone. Both my hands circled those mounds, and I squeezed them, kneading the color into the skin.

"I bent once more and applied the rouge to the hair in her groin, stroking gently, allowing my fingers to follow the bend of her body and to trail into the hot, wet groove below.

"'I think we are ready now,' she said and turned away.

"'Ready?' I repeated foolishly.

"'For the pictures, of course.'

"'The pictures will come later,' I said.

"'No, no,' she smiled. 'The pictures will come now.' She lay down on the sofa. 'Please bring me a glass of wine, Peter.'

"'No.'

"'Please…and then we'll see about the pictures.'

"I went into the next room, poured two glasses of wine, and then started back to the studio. But I stopped, put the glasses back upon the table, and stripped myself of all my clothing. I can't tell you what a relief it was to allow my howling penis its freedom from being pressed against clothing. So, undressed, I picked up the glasses again and, as I was about to enter the studio, I paused dead in the doorway, unable to move or to speak, for the most incredible little scene was being enacted before my eyes.

"Clara still lay on the sofa, her skin exquisite with

powder, her nipples glowing with rouge, and she was looking across the studio at the door that leads to the anteroom. She was so casual I could not believe she saw what I saw there. It was a fairly short, well-built boy of about eighteen, his large black eyes staring wildly at Clara. He wore a T-shirt and, at first, I thought he was otherwise completely naked, but then I saw he was wearing briefs. The three of us merely stared without moving, until suddenly the boy drove his fingers through his shock of black hair, then put both hands to the band of his briefs and pulled them down his hips. His penis burst out, large and inflamed.

"'You like it?' he shouted across at her, his voice echoing in the studio.

"'Yes, yes, yes," she shouted back at him. Her legs shot wide apart, so wide her beautiful pussy gaped at me.

"The boy tore his shirt off, pulled his briefs down his legs and lunged across the room, flinging himself with a jump on top of Clara. Their mouths were open and they slammed against each other. I saw Clara's arm twist until her hand reached the boy's member. Drawing her knees back, she held the head of his cock against her opening, and with one thrust the boy drove himself all the way into her. Bouncing, pumping, swinging, grinding—they went at it like devils.

"I flung the glasses of wine to the floor and raced to the sofa, my prick flopping ridiculously.

"'Stop it,' I cried. 'What are you doing?'

"But they ignored me, continuing to bang themselves as if I didn't exist. I grabbed the boy's shoulder and tried to pull him away from Clara, but her legs moved until they circled his back and she kept him in place. Standing beside them, I shouted,

'Stop it, stop it,' and was torn between rage and passion. They had both begun to moan, and his penis made a sucking sound as it dug in and out of her juicy sheath. Clara shrieked and the boy dropped motionless upon her; there was no longer any sound but their hoarse breathing.

"Taking hold of his shoulder again I pulled at him and this time managed to dislodge him and bring him to his feet. His tool was shiny with Clara's juices.

"'How did you get in here?' I asked him.

"He stared at me dumbly and then down at his still-dripping rod, the sight of which infuriated me even further.

"'Answer me,' I roared. 'How did you get in here?'

"'Through the door,' he said.

"'Who are you?'

"'Nobody.'

"'Tell me who you are!'

"'I'll tell you who he is,' Clara said lazily.

"I turned upon her. 'You filthy whore. Would you let anyone who walked through that door fuck you?'

"'No, not anyone, Peter.' She seemed offended. 'But he's so cute. Come here, darling,' she beckoned to the boy. 'Let's do it again.'

"He turned toward her, his cock stiffening.

"'No, you won't do it again. Put your clothes on and get out of here.'

"'Me?' Clara asked smiling.

"'No, not you. I'll take care of you as soon as he's gone.' I looked at the boy. 'Get out.'

"'I don't want to,' he said. 'I want more of that.' And he brazenly put his hand on Clara's muff.

"'That's enough,' she told him. 'You'd better leave now. I've got to save a little for Peter.'

"'I won't leave.'

"'Yes you will,' she said, removing his hand from between her thighs. 'If you don't, you'll never have any more from me.'

"'All right, I'll go, but just let me suck you a little." He knelt beside the sofa and his face disappeared into her valley of delight.

"'I won't have this,' I said.

"'Oh, be quiet, Peter, and come here. Yes, yes, come here.'

"I obeyed, leaning against the sofa until the tip of my cock poked against Clara's sweet red mouth. She moved her head, forcing my rod deeper, always deeper. The warmth tugged at my blood, and her tongue circling around made me shiver. Relinquishing my organ, she put her mouth to my scrotum and lapped playfully in short strokes. I edged around and threw myself on top of her, giving the boy a sudden thrust as I dropped. He fell back to the floor and I found that now my face was at a level with Clara's groin. Moving downward, I felt her insert my penis in her mouth once more, and at the same moment my face went between her thighs and before my eyes lay only the quivering pink flesh, aflame with the syrups of pleasure—a world of ripe odors, of curling hair, of heavy moisture. My tongue went up and down, eating and drinking at Clara's full table. I bit at her gently and felt her bites return mine along the length of my shaft. My tongue dug into her canal, flickered in and out until everything shuddered, went hot and cold. My mouth was not big enough to enclose all the delights Clara could offer.

"Meanwhile, Clara licked me until I thought I would lose all control. She was an expert. Her tongue swirled around the head of my cock and teased it until it was red and swollen. Then she swallowed me to the balls, bobbing her head up and down while she maintained a pressure on my shaft that I felt sure would milk it of every drop of sperm. She stroked the ridge along the underside of my lance and then flicked at my balls. I was moments away from coming. Suddenly she pushed my member from her.

"'Fuck me, now, Peter. Fuck me,' she sighed.

"I lifted my face and turned my body around. Our faces met violently, mouths grinding together, tongues flung deep into each other. I felt her legs draw up under me and her cavern was arched against my throbbing organ. With one jolt, it was in—inserted deep within her. Legs went around my back, squeezing me so tightly I could barely breathe. My hands clutched at her breasts, tugging at them, molding them, and our mouths never parted. Her hips began to sway slightly, and my own joined in with her motion. We rocked back and forth gently; then gradually I began to circle my penis in her. Ultimately I began drawing it in and out in long movements, slowly taking it out as far as the head, then plunging back deep, endlessly. She was shaking with passion and I sensed that her moment was near. My thrusts became shorter and faster, but always I dug deep in her as if I must break the walls of her sheath. Each thrust made her moan and her tongue ran wild in my mouth. Our moment came together—one maddening instant when our teeth ground and we were the dripping movements of our loins. I shot my burning flood of sperm into her in four great, shuddering gouts, while the pearly nectar of her passion inundated my shaft.

"Afterwards, we lay breathing heavily.

"'Now it's my turn,' I heard the boy say.

"I refused to answer him.

"'Get up,' he said to me. 'If you don't let me fuck her I'll fuck *you*'

"I still wouldn't reply, but then abruptly I realized he meant what he'd said, for he jumped on top of me and was trying to drive his penis into my anus. Twisting myself, I made him drop to the floor again, and I pulled myself to my feet.

"'Get out of here,' I said.

"'Let him stay, Peter,' said Clara.

"'No, I don't want him here.'

"'Don't you think I've got enough for both of you?'

"'That isn't the point. I won't have a strange kid barging in here and playing around with my woman.'

"'*Your* woman,' the boy sneered. 'As it happens I got into *your* woman before *you* did.'

"'How do you know that?' I asked.

"'I told him, Peter.'

"'You mean you knew him before tonight?'

"'Yes,' she laughed. 'I met him last week on the way back from your place one night. He thought he was going to rape me and dragged me into the courtyard of a building. Of course I could have screamed, but he didn't seem to be violent and his cock was wonderfully long, so I only fought and scratched. The next thing I knew he'd torn my blouse open and ripped my panties off and had his tool between my legs. It was something different and wonderfully exciting to see the unrestrained heat of his passion as he thought he was having his own way. He had my arms pinned with his and his knees separating my thighs as he rammed into me. I lay back and moaned—though I didn't need to simulate the pleasure I felt—and pretended to squirm and wriggle. This excited him even more and he plunged his hot tool into me again and again. The scenario so thrilled me that even though he shot his cream into me within a few seconds I was right behind him with my own orgasm. It was a wonderful diversion.

"'I gave you a good fuck, didn't I?' he asked.

"'You always do, Jean. And Peter gave me a good one too. How marvelous to have two wonderful men, one warming up just as the other is cooling off.'

"This arrangement may have been wonderful for Clara, but it was not the sort of thing that amused me. 'So you think the party is going to be for the three of us every night?' I asked her.

"'Why not?'

"'Well, I won't have it. You could have gone on meeting him at some other time and certainly some other place. What was the idea of bringing him here?'

"'Well, if you want to know the truth—'

"'Of course, I do.'

"'I wanted to get you jealous. I wanted to see you go as crazy as you've been driving me these past weeks. Every night I'd get steamed up and then you…you did nothing but take pictures. The night I met Jean I was so hot I could barely walk down the street. You can imagine how hot we must have been to start rolling on the concrete of a courtyard on a cold night. I had it all planned for him to come here the night the color film arrived. I thought I'd get you really worked up, and when you were most excited Jean would appear and it would happen just as it happened.'

"'But how could he get in with the door locked?' I asked.

"'It wasn't locked,' she said. 'I released the latch when you weren't looking and I'd warned him to come in quietly, undress to his underwear, and then wait until he heard me send you for wine. At that point he was to come in. I suppose I don't have to explain the rest.'

"Jean was apparently uninterested in all the talk and he held his erect penis in his hand as if reining it in. The swollen head jutted above his fist like a ripe plum.

"'Let me give it to you, Clara,' he said. 'I want to fuck you. And I know you want me to ram it in your pussy.'

"'Yes, yes.' She closed her eyes and waited.

"As he had before, he jumped and flung himself upon her.

"'Let's do it,' she said, 'with me on top of you this time.'

"'And what am I supposed to do?' I asked.

"'You can take pictures of us,' Jean answered. 'There's good money in these pictures. I can sell them for you.'

"'Oh, yes, Peter. Take pictures—in color. But wait, we'll have to put makeup on Jean.'

"She left the sofa and brought the paint chest over to the boy. She applied the makeup to his face then powdered his body with the same care I had taken in powdering hers.

"'We'll put some rouge on your cock,' she said, 'although it's red enough now.'

"She applied the color to her own lips and then, by putting her mouth over Jean's member, she transferred the color to him. Then she evened out the rouge by licking at his penis with her tongue. She licked a great deal, making most of the paint disappear, so she was forced to begin the process again. She applied the color heavily to her lips and then took Jean's cock in her mouth. Only this time she seemed less concerned with spreading the rouge evenly over his throbbing tool than with swallowing his meat. The color streaked over his swollen cock-head and shaft as she took him down her throat and licked at his balls. She popped them one at a time into her mouth and sucked them gently, then returned to laving the shaft until she'd managed to at least deposit some of the color where it belonged. While doing this, she knelt on the floor and slid my head between her thighs. She pressed down against me and her cunt seemed thicker than before as it filled my mouth. I sucked her passionately, licking up and down the slit and nibbling her clitoris, and brought my hands round to fondle her buttocks. My fingers trailed into the crevice between her cheeks and I tickled her anus, which began to widen. Breaking away from her, I took a jar of cream from the makeup chest and smoothed it into her butthole. Then, kneeling in back of her, I drove my aching prick into her hole. My arms circled round her, one hand digging into her flooded pussy and the other squeezing her breasts, and all the time she continued sucking the boy. I thrilled with the oily sensation of the cream and the tightness of this new hole. She kept forcing her buttocks back upon me; the pressure made me wild and I lunged in and out savagely, pulling at her cunt with my fingers. The sensation of her soft bottomcheeks thrashing me as I pounded into her was excruciating. The sight of my glistening tool diving into her asshole time and again was so thrilling that I could feel my flood rising from my balls after just a few strokes. My cock swelled still more and became wedged tightly in her orifice as I blasted my sperm into her. After three or four spasms my tool diminished sufficiently for me to remove it and I fell weakly away from her. Clara, of course, was ready for more.

"'Well, the makeup's on,' she said, rising away

from me. 'Now, we've got to try some pictures. You tell us how to pose.'

"There was no need to tell them anything, for they both seemed quite expert at posing. I took a great many photographs that night, and when it was time to rest, the only change was that Jean climbed off Clara, and I climbed on. Toward dawn, Clara said she had to leave, but Jean decided he liked my flat and thought he might stay for a few days.

"'You will not stay here for a few days or even a few minutes. It may be possible to tolerate you for the pleasure of Clara, but when she's not here, I don't want you here either.'

"Since we continued arguing, Clara dressed and left the apartment without waiting for the results of the discussion. Still naked, Jean and I argued. Finally he lay down on the sofa and pretended he had gone to sleep. I shook him, but he would not respond.

"'You're not deceiving me,' I said. 'You'll have to get out of here.'

"A little smile came to his face and I noticed that his penis had become erect again. He turned around suddenly and buried his face in my crotch. His tongue sought my prick. I backed away.

"'If you let me stay here,' he said, 'you'll be able to have fun even when Clara's not around.'

"He reached out and fondled my member, and when it stiffened, put it into his mouth. He sucked as well as Clara, and doubtless had had as much experience at it as she. He licked the head and shaft and spent a longer time ministering to my balls. I was horrified at first, then relaxed as the pleasant sensations overcame my resistance. After several moments of this, Jean reached for the makeup cream and spread some on my cock. Then he bent over and pushed back—and my hand guided my penis between his buttocks and into its new home.

"And so, he stayed the night. He stayed in fact, for the next two weeks and the three of us enjoyed great pleasures during those nights. Unfortunately, Jean saw to it I had my pleasures during the day as well, and it was perhaps best that it all finally ended—or I might have been a wrecked man. I can remember no period of my life when I was in such a state of exhaustion as the last days of the two weeks with Clara and Jean.

"The color photographs of the two of them making love came out reasonably well, especially the close-ups, and Jean did, as he had promised, sell them for me. This brought me more money than I'd ever had before and also began the career I practice to this very day. Doubtless Jean cheated me out of much of the money, but I could not complain since he was willing to model and what he left me was more than adequate for my needs.

"It was primarily jealousy that broke up this happy arrangement of sex and money. Clara was jealous because Jean was more interested in pleasing me than in pleasing her; I was jealous that Clara cared so much about Jean; and, finally, Jean was jealous because when Clara was present I preferred to fill her openings rather than his. This last jealousy kept me rooted in Jean's asshole practically all the time when Clara was absent—and was the chief reason for my fatigue. At last, the three of us had a row and we ended by actually fighting. Clara dressed and stormed out swearing she would never come back. The moment she was gone Jean rushed at me laughing and delighted.

"'Now, there's only the two of us,' he said.

"'Yes, and that's too many.'

"'What do you mean?'

"'I mean, you'll have to go. And I won't put up with any discussion.'

"'Have you forgotten our wonderful afternoons—just the two of us?'

"'No, unfortunately, I haven't forgotten.'

"'Weren't they wonderful?'

"'It was interesting for two weeks. But I'm afraid going to bed with you all the time isn't quite my taste.'

"He fell to his knees—we were both naked—and began sucking my penis.

"'Stop it,' I said. 'You'll have to go.'

"But he continued, and I could see he had begun to cry. It was difficult to believe that this tearful boy licking my cock was the same one who had raped Clara. He took me down his throat and pumped me with a frenzy born of desperation. In any case, I flung him away. He returned and I pushed him again, harder than I intended. Coming back, he deliberately provoked me into hitting him, and he continued to do so. We both became a little wild, and I pounded him with all my strength. It was a while before I realized how he had manipulated me and how much he was enjoying it. He moaned and sighed; his penis was in an enormous state of erection. I'd gone so far I couldn't stop, and I continued beating him, pinching him, tearing at him until he was bloody. With each wound inflicted, his passion rose, and he rubbed against my body like a devoted pet. He dropped into a heap at my feet, begging me to kick him, and I did, again and again. Each time he came back to stroke, lick, kiss my ankles, knees, prick or thighs. Half-crazy, I threw myself on him, my own cock rigid and throbbing. His buttocks rose under me, and suddenly we were locked together, though I don't know how it was accomplished. While we rolled and swayed I continued pounding him as if this last horrible act would purge me of all the terrible degeneracy of the past two weeks. My cock pistoned in and out of his ass, tearing at him, and finally I came in a rush.

"I was so revolted afterwards that I couldn't look at him. He begged and pleaded with me all that day and into the next night, while I waited for Clara. She never returned. I refused to talk to Jean or look at him. Twenty-four hours later he was gone.

"Clara never came back, and except for one short note I never heard from or of her again. A week after she left, she sent me a letter saying she hoped I would remember to make the package of photographs up for you. And she asked two other things, one of which I was not to tell you immediately. The other was—well, Mr. Cunningham, that you would pose for a picture."

Van Drooft looked at me rather shyly.

"Of course I'd pose for a picture. Although I can't—"

"I mean a picture in the nude. The kind of picture I took of Clara."

"Why would she have wanted me to—"

"That is what I am not to tell you immediately. The whole thing shouldn't take more than a few moments. It is the least either of us can do toward the memory of such a passionate woman."

"Yes, all right. I agree. Let's just get it over with."

"If you'll just wait a minute, I'll bring the package. It should be in the back somewhere. Please help yourself to some more wine."

When he had gone, I stood up to pour some wine. It was then I noticed the enormous shadow of Colette at the door leading into the studio. I moved and saw her, dress up, hands between her thighs tugging hotly at her mountainous flesh. She seemed embarrassed but didn't stop what she was doing.

"I couldn't help—I overheard the story and it excited me. Will you fuck me, Mr. Cunningham?"

She threw her dress over her head and came to me, waving her arms, her enormous breasts sagging, her thick thighs scraping together. I was so startled and repulsed I might have struck her, but at that moment Van Drooft returned.

"They were easier to find than I thought—" He stopped short. "Ah, I see Colette is ready for the photograph. I hope you don't mind, Mr. Cunningham. It would be difficult to get another female at this time of day. And it's best to do the thing right now."

"I'm not sure…"

"It will all be over in a minute."

Colette smiled rapturously and came to help me undress. She was not very helpful because her hands were concentrated on my fly, but finally I managed to get out of my clothes.

"You have such a nice cock," said Colette. "But it's so itty-bitty. We have to make it big for the photograph, don't we?"

I encountered the same difficulty the young man had had earlier that afternoon when he was faced with the prospect of getting an erection over Colette.

"Perhaps this will help," said van Drooft as he handed me some pictures he had taken of Clara and Jean. It was rather a shock to see her again, just as she had been twenty years ago. But I succumbed to the memory of her flesh and my penis rose—Colette still laboring at it maddeningly.

In the studio, Colette eased onto the sofa and I climbed on top of her. It was much more pleasant than I'd imagined. My cock sank deep into her pussy. She drew her legs wide and back and I edged my rod back and forth through the meaty mound. She was so large my cock didn't have to fully penetrate her for my balls to be resting against her buttocks.

"Don't put all of it in," said van Drooft. "Now, hold it."

The camera clicked once, twice, and twice more.

"That's all," said van Drooft. "I'll develop it now." And he was gone.

"You can put all of it in now," Colette whispered. She lumbered her hips until I found my penis lodged in her pastry.

She was all wet and soft. I fondled her breasts, round and flabby like loaves of unbaked bread. I bent my head and worried the expansive nipples with my teeth.

"Oh, oh, oh," she whimpered and moved her hips so quickly that my penis was milked and tensed for its spurt.

Colette wanted more, but I considered it quite enough and pulled out of her before I came. I left her to dress. When I had my clothing on, van Drooft came back and handed me the photograph. The shock of it made my heart pound. Clara had asked Van Drooft to superimpose a picture of me on one of her. So I had replaced Jean on this photograph, and Clara had replaced Colette. One half was faded and one half was fresh, but the area where my half-inserted penis entered her half-filled womanhood was so clear it might have been photographed yesterday.

CHAPTER FOUR

IV.

It was not until several hours after I left van Drooft's studio that I began to react to the story he had told me. For a while I thought I could not fulfill Clara's last request—or, at least, fulfill it any further. Already in van Drooft's story, I could see the roots of Clara's promise to go crazy beginning to take hold. I wanted to go no further, to hear no more. Yet, was it more painful to listen to than to have lived? The second half of her life was to be in part a revenge against my disloyalty. Was I to deprive her of this revenge? Clearly, I could, and since she was dead it could hardly matter. But in the midst of the anguish I felt, I *knew* that I must go through with it, just as she had gone through with it.

I drank late into the night, but did not succeed in getting myself drunk or even numb. Eventually I went to bed, my bones aching, and I slept badly. I slept, dreamed and woke; then re-slept, re-dreamed, and re-woke; and then again. Nightmares brought me awake with sounds coming from my throat. In each of the dreams, Clara walked along a street full of gaping people. She was naked and her body was painted like a rainbow. I followed her, and she avoided me, but she always looked to see if I were there. At that point in the dream I decided I could reach her. I'd begun to run.

"Howard," she'd call.

"Yes, I'm coming."

"Howard..."

"I'll catch you."

"Howard..."

"Don't move. Stay there."

"Howard..."

"Yes, Clara, yes."

"Howard..."

She began to laugh, and laughing, fell to the ground with her legs wide apart.

"Howard..."

"Your cunt, Clara. Your beautiful cunt. It smells like pastry. I want it."

"Howard..."

I ran to her, ran and ran, getting no closer.

"Howard..."

"I'll bite into your pastry."

"Howard..."

"Here I am. I'm coming. We'll fuck savagely."

"Howard..."

Suddenly, in every dream, I was before her. Her legs went wider and what lay between them invited me. I was naked and my erection kept growing. It grew, as it were, for acres and acres, and as it reached her loins I realized I was burying my penis in a nest of snakes. There were a million snakes crawling in her womanhood. I leaped back, pulling my penis in like a telescope.

"Howard..."

But I'd come no closer.

"Howard…"

The snakes grew, tangled, their tongues flickered in and out, lapping toward me.

"Howard…"

I stood utterly horrified, but refused to help her. The snakes were enormous now and had begun to twist round her body.

"Howard!" she screamed, horrified. "Howard! Howard! Howard! Howard!"

And I woke from the dream, groaning. But only to fall asleep again, repeat the nightmare, and awake once more. At dawn, I washed my face and smoked a cigarette, exhausted from my terrible night. I tried once more to sleep, and this time I was more successful. I slept dreamlessly until the afternoon.

The next name on Clara's list was Jean Dupont. I wondered if it could be the same Jean that van Drooft had talked about the day before. His address was that of a hotel in the Pigalle area. Since Clara had listed no telephone number for the hotel and since I could find no number for it in the directory, I drove up to Pigalle at about six o'clock that evening, wound my car around the small back streets, and finally reached the hotel.

It was freshly painted and had an air of false respectability. The reception desk was at such an angle that anyone could easily go up the stairs without being observed. Clearly, this was a place that rented rooms by the hour. Walking to the desk, I hit the bell, but no one came. It took a good deal of ringing to get a rather old man down the stairs.

"Yes?" he asked.

"Can you tell me if there's someone here named Jean Dupont?"

"No, there's no one here by that name."

"But he has lived here."

"I couldn't tell you." He started back up the steps.

"Wait a minute. Couldn't you check? Perhaps there's a forwarding address."

"No. No forwarding address."

I took a thousand-franc note out of my wallet and placed it on the desk.

He came down the stairs quickly and grabbed the money.

"Dupont hasn't lived here for some time. But he has a little friend upstairs. Maybe she can help you. Name's Rose. Her room number is 17—third floor, to your right."

"Thanks very much."

"At your service."

I climbed to the third floor and found the room—the door slightly ajar, the interior very dark. I thought that Rose might be too occupied to provide me with any information at that particular moment, but I listened, and hearing no noise, I rapped at the door. A woman's hoarse voice mumbled something which I thought was an invitation to enter, so I did and closed the door behind me. In the dim light of the room—the windows were heavily draped—I saw the plump naked form of a woman on the bed.

"Did you get it?" she asked me, then suddenly sat up. "Hey, who are you?"

"I'm terribly sorry." I smiled. She frowned but didn't bother to cover herself. In the red-toned darkness of the room, her flesh looked like a ripe fruit. Every part of her body glowed with ripeness, maturity. Her breasts were not too large, but they swelled out firmly and ended in jutting brown nipples. Her arms and legs had a meaty softness. The thick moss between her thighs was a whispered invitation. She was the kind of woman that oozes sex all along her body.

"Get out of here and come back later," she said. "He'll kill you if he sees you here."

"Jean?"

"Not Jean, Pierre. Say, who are you? How do you know Jean?"

"I don't. I'm—"

"Shut up." She jumped out of the bed in a panic. "He's coming up the stairs. Oh my God."

I started to the door, but she stopped me. "Go behind that screen and for God's sake don't breathe. I'll send him out again for a minute and then you can leave."

I was hardly behind the screen when I heard the door open.

"Here's the wine," said Pierre harshly. "It's so damn warm out."

"Oh, Pierre," said Rose, "I know it's warm. But would you mind going out once more for your sweet little girl?"

"I don't want to go out. I'm going to fuck you now."

"In a minute. Couldn't you go down and bring me an aspirin? I have a terrible headache."

"I'll take your headache away. I have just the pill for it."

"I have such an awful headache. Please get me an aspirin."

"If you don't shut up, I'll make your headache go away. And I'll make your head go away with it." He sounded like he meant it.

"Please…" Rose begged, and then there was the frightening sound of hand meeting flesh. Rose shrieked, then began sobbing. I assumed it would be some time before I could make my escape, so I loosened my collar and looked around at my whereabouts. There was a sink and a bidet within sight of me. I hoped Pierre had no intention of using either. Since there was nothing else to do, I settled myself down on the bidet and listened to their conversation.

"Get on that bed and stop crying!"

"But my head…"

"Didn't you have enough? You want more?"

"No. No, honey," soothed Rose. "Only I want to be so nice to you, and I won't be at my best when I have a headache.

"You better be at your best. Now, get on that bed."

There was a sound of springs; and Pierre grunting as he got out of his clothes.

"Everything's sticking to me, it's so damn hot. You going to stick to me?"

"Sure, honey. Going to stick to you like glue, wheedled Rose. "Only my head…"

"Enough about your head," roared Pierre. "Here, let me rub this pill against your head. It's a nice warm pill."

"Oh, it's a good pill. But pills have to be swallowed, don't they?"

"That's right."

Suddenly I heard sucking sounds and the pole between my legs began to stiffen.

"Wouldn't you like to swallow my pill?" said Rose.

"No, I won't swallow it, but I'll chew it up."

Sucking sounds began again, joined by the grunts and sighs of the two lovers.

"Ah, that's good…Yes…there…bite it…harder…oh, Pierre."

"What a cunt!"

"All yours, Pierre…Put your tongue in…around and around…deeper…ah…ah…I'm…all aching…

I'm all one piece of aching cunt...so hard and hot...oh, oh, oh...again...bite me there again."

"Don't pull me so fast, you'll make me come. Yes, that's good. Yes, gently. Put your lips there again."

"Oh, Pierre, fuck me, fuck me. I'll go crazy. Here, you lie down."

"I want to eat your tits. Put that thick brown nipple in my mouth."

"There...oh, bite it, Pierre...kill me, Pierre, chew me to pieces."

"Enough of that. Come and sit on me. That's right. Squat over it. Now lower yourself slowly. More. It's going in."

"I know, I know," gasped Rose. "Its enormous helmet is piercing into me."

"Lower yourself some more. More. It's almost in. All the way. Press yourself down all the way."

Rose was obviously having difficulty breathing, for her words came haltingly. "All of it is in me now. Your whole column is filling me, burning me...Do you want me to move?"

"A little...move a little...that's right...slowly, up and down."

"Oh, oh, it's slipping out...in...it's a mountain tearing in and out of me...I feel it beating, throbbing, in me...yes, do that...oh, Pierre, do that...move like that...oh, in again...quickly! push it more...oh, wonderful...and your balls hot against my ass."

"Up, up. Move quickly. I'll grab your tits. Move quickly. Quickly."

"Quickly...quickly...it's steaming in me...if it gets any harder I'll burst open...oh, now, again, again, again...break me open, destroy me...those balls...that cock..."

"Your cunt full of grease...I'm coming."

"Come...lunge...plunge, faster, faster...oh, I'll

die…of…crazy…faster…your…hot cock…oh, oh…
owww…"

"I'm coming," grunted Pierre. "I'm coming."

"Ohhh…"

There were a few minutes of silence.

"Put your filthy cunt in my face. I want to drink
what I just filled you with."

"How wet I am. You've drowned me with your boil-
ing sperm. Oh, fuck me again. I can't bear to be without your cock in me. Let me lie down now. Come on
top of me. Drop your body on me. Suffocate me. Oh,
how heavy you are."

"You're so soft. I'm falling deep into you. Your
pussy is taking me in."

"Let me take your cock in. Put your cock in. Yes, all
the way. Oh, it's wonderful. Make me come again.
Don't wait! Pump, pump! Yes! Bounce on me—jump
on me!"

"Put your legs up around me," ordered Pierre.
"Move your behind. Good."

"Hurry! I can't wait! I must have it…oh…like that."

"Lord, I'm coming again! My cock is going to
burst."

"Yes, fill me again. I feel it storming in me.
More…more…more…more…kiss me, Pierre…kiss
me…"

There were stifled moans; sighs; the slurp of their
kiss, the squishing sound of his penis moving in her.

"That was so good," she murmured. "I could do it
all night."

"We will."

In fact, I was becoming desperate that they might. It
might not have been so bad if I could see what was
going on. But my view was completely obscured.
Obviously Rose had forgotten about me. To remind
her, I made a slight scratching sound at the screen.

"What was that?" asked Pierre.

"I—I don't hear anything."

"I heard a noise."

"It's probably the water pipes. Oh, Pierre, my head is worse. Couldn't you get me an aspirin?"

"You want me to get dressed now? If I get dressed, I won't come back, and you can fuck yourself the rest of the night."

"Oh, no, Pierre. You wouldn't leave. Just put your trousers on and ask at the desk for an aspirin. Please. And then we'll have wine and start again."

"All right," he said without enthusiasm. I heard him slip into his clothes and then the door opened and closed.

"Hey, you," hissed Rose. "Quick, get out."

I came from behind the screen.

"You got some earful," she said.

She was standing up and I couldn't resist driving my hand between her legs; the hot dripping flesh thrilled me. I dug a finger into her slit and frigged her quickly. She closed her eyes for a moment, then seemed to come to her senses.

"Come some other time. I've got enough for all."

"Tell me where I can find Jean Dupont."

"Why?"

"I'm an old friend of his."

"You sure you're not a cop?"

I wriggled my hand in her pussy and grabbed one of her tits.

"Does that feel like I'm a cop?" I asked.

"Cops like to fuck too."

She whispered the address to me and then pushed me out the door, giving me an affectionate goodbye by pulling at the bulge in my trousers.

As I walked down the steps, Pierre was coming up. He was shirtless and shoeless, a hulking brute of about thirty-five. He looked at me menacingly as I passed, and then continued up the stairs.

Since the address Rose had given me was that of a hotel only a very short distance away, I didn't bother taking my car. I walked back to the boulevard and south a couple of blocks and then turned left, right, and left. I emerged on a fairly broad, light, pleasant-looking street. The hotel itself was not so freshly painted as the other had been, but it was obviously of much better quality. It was more a place for tourists than sordid affairs.

At the desk, an elderly woman adjusted her glasses and smiled at me.

"I'd like to speak to Jean Dupont, please."

"I'll ring his room," she said. She picked up the phone and dialed a number. "Monsieur Dupont? There's a gentleman here to see you." She turned to me. "What did you say your name was?"

"Cunningham. Tell him I'm an American."

She told him. "Yes, Monsieur Dupont. Yes, I'll tell him." She replaced the receiver and turned to me. "He's coming right down, Mr. Cunningham. Would you take a seat in the lobby?"

I went into the lobby, sat down, lit a cigarette, and looked around the room. Less than five minutes later, Dupont came down. He was a short, dark, stocky, young-looking man, rather handsome, and he was extremely well-dressed. Coming into the lobby, he smiled at me.

"Mr. Cunningham?"

"That's right."

"What can I do for you, sir?"

"I wonder if we might go out for a drink. My errand is a little odd to discuss here."

Curiously, he winked at me. "Fine," he said. "Where would you like to go?"

"Anywhere. Somewhere quiet."

"There's a nice little café not far from here."

We left the hotel and went round the corner to a fairly large café that faced on a square. Since it was approaching the dinner hour, the terrace of the café was deserted.

"Would you like to sit out here?" he asked me.

"Yes."

We sat down and when the waiter came I ordered for both of us.

"Now, I'll tell you why I've looked you up."

"No need to tell me. Do you want a man, woman, or child?"

"For what?"

He looked at me with some bewilderment. "Say, who gave you my address?"

"I was just about to tell you. It was Clara."

"Clara who? Aren't you the American I expected this afternoon?"

"No, I'm afraid not."

The extreme politeness he had shown me until now disappeared at once. "Who are you?"

"You know my name. I've come at the request of Clara."

"I don't know any Clara. Are you sure you're not a cop?"

"How could I be a cop? I'm an American."

"How do I know that? I think I'll say goodnight."

"Wait a minute. Look here." I handed him my passport. He flipped through the pages.

"It looks real," he said.

"It *is* real."

He leaned over. "How much you want for it?"

"For the passport?"

"Sure."

"Sorry, it's not for sale."

"A hundred thousand francs?"

"I assure you," I said sternly, "it's not for sale."

"Well, what the hell do you want from me then?"

"Information."

"So you *are* a cop." He made as if to get up from the table, and I put my hand on his arm.

"Listen, Dupont, the information I want is of use to no one but myself. In fact, it isn't even of any actual use to *me* and I'm after it only for sentimental reasons."

"I'll bet," he laughed.

"Do you remember a woman named Clara?"

"No."

"A very beautiful woman."

"Look, friend, I deal in beautiful women."

"This one was young and had platinum hair. Perhaps you knew her at a time when she was friendly with the photographer named van Drooft."

He looked at me incredulously and said, "Clara. Oh, my God, you mean Clara."

"That's what I said."

"I haven't see her since before the war."

"She's dead."

"I didn't know that."

"She died a few days ago. The fact is, she left a letter for me in which she listed a number of names and addresses. Yours was one of them. She asked me to go around to see these people and to ask them about their relations with her."

"What did she want you to do that for?"

"To be perfectly frank, it's a form of revenge. Clara and I were in love; when we broke up, she warned me of the kind of life she'd lead if we separated. Now, I think, she wants me to make good on her promise."

Dupont nodded his head and smiled. "Say, you must be that man who ran out on her."

"If you want to put it that way—"

"Sure, she told me about you. She said you'd come by one day to ask about her. Well, what do you want to know?"

"Anything you'd care to tell me about Clara."

Staring thoughtfully into his drink, he seemed to be considering what he ought to tell me.

"Did you say you know van Drooft?"

"I only met him yesterday. His was the first name on the list."

"Lousy little pansy, he is."

"Is that so?"

"Yes. I was fucking him day and night, and Clara, too. They could never get enough of it. I finally had to get away from both of them or I would have dried up and died."

At that point, he recounted more or less the same tale van Drooft had told me, only the homosexual element was completely reversed. It was van Drooft who had begged Dupont to stay on at the studio; the trio broke up because Dupont found it physically impossible to keep both his concubines satisfied; van Drooft was the one who had begged to be beaten and had so disgusted Dupont that the latter walked out on him. Which of the two versions was the true one, I cannot say at all. Besides, it was of little relevance in relation to Clara. One thing was certain: she was not playing husband to either of them. Whoever was the pot, Clara was not the potter.

I pick up Dupont's story where van Drooft left off:

"Well, after I told van Drooft to go to hell, I left his apartment, and I didn't want to have anything more to do with him. But I didn't feel I was finished with Clara. I wanted more of her. Still, I decided not to go back to the studio, so for the next week or so I went to the building where van Drooft lived. I went there about midnight, and every night I waited an hour or so. Sometimes while I was waiting, van Drooft came out of the building and went down the street. So it seemed pretty certain that Clara wasn't interested anymore. I knew she was interested in me, but where was I going to find her? She didn't know my address, and I didn't know hers.

"Finally, I got fed up and stopped coming around to van Drooft's. I didn't see Clara again for almost five years—until the spring of 1938. During those five years, I got established in a nice little business. I went into the meat trade. I'd had some experience at it from the time I was a kid, but just about the time I lost track of Clara, I went into it seriously. It was pretty easy. I had a lot of gorgeous girls who were nuts about me—and I started thinking, well, why not make a profit out of it? So what I did was, I'd tell the girls that if they expected me to fuck them, they'd have to do me little favors in return. Some of them agreed right away, and some of them had to sit around a while and realize what they were missing before they came around. I'll tell you, when a girl's been fucked by Jean Dupont, she stays fucked, and no one else satisfies her. That goes for guys like van Drooft, too. You know why I'm living in the hotel I am and wearing these clothes? Because there are sixty-six women, men, boys, and girls all over Paris who'll do anything I say just to get a fuck out of me. And naturally they don't any of them get it more than once every two or three months. So, because I fuck them half-a-dozen times a year, they spend the rest of the year being fucked by the people I send to them. Half of them don't even need the money—and they don't get it. They do it for love of me.

He laughed. "My oldest woman is 92. She's the best cock-sucker in Paris and, maybe, all of France. She's a rich, crazy old babe with a big house in a ritzy part of the city. I tell you, you haven't had a wild night until you've been sucked by her.

"And then there's my old man, who's 88 next month. He wouldn't be much in demand except he's got the biggest collection of whips in the world, and he's raring to use them.

"But those are only two of my employees. There are sixty-six others, all devoted. Of course, business hasn't always been so good. For a long time I had to content myself with a handful of women and a couple of men. But now I've got a suite at the hotel and a house in the country. Things couldn't be better.

"As I was saying, for the four-and-a-half or five years when I didn't see Clara I was all the time building up my little empire, and I didn't have much time to think of her. Actually, I was always busy walking around trying to get people to fall in love with me, so I could make money out of them. Well, as it happened, I was doing the outskirts of Paris that night, and I was going around the cafés at Vincennes. When I'd reached the edge of the woods, I saw a taxi stop about ten feet ahead of me, and out stepped Clara, as beautiful as ever. She'd filled out a little and her tits were so swollen and ripe I would've eaten them there in the street. A man got out with her. He was rather elderly and he kept moving his hands in front of him to hide the lump in his pants.

"Clara didn't notice me, and she and the old guy were starting for the woods. I followed them, keeping a distance, and I had a wonderful idea. When they were pretty deep in the wood, they stopped at a small clearing and started kissing like crazy. I could hear the old man wheezing and tearing at Clara's dress.

Clara

Finally they both got undressed, and I almost dropped a load just looking at her. What a girl! Her tits were unbelievably full and round. The nipples projected a full inch from the ends. Her hips were lush and the moss between her thighs was a siren song. She lay down on the ground and spread her legs wide. The man kept walking around her, looking at her, holding his cock in his hands.

"This is no time for looking, I thought. And quickly, just like the time at van Drooft's, I got undressed back in the trees where I was hidden. I stripped down to my briefs and my undershirt, and I walked out into the clearing. Clara saw me and just stared. So I pulled my briefs down to below my balls and my rod stuck out in the air like a flagpole.

"'You like it?' I yelled at her.

"'Yes, yes, yes,' she shrieked.

"I tore my things off and went bounding across the clearing and lunged so that I fell square on top of her, knocking the breath out of both of us.

"'Jean,' she whimpered, 'Jean, it's been so long...'

"'It's still long,' I told her. She began twitching and pulled her legs back so her twat was smack against my cock. I rubbed against her hard. I never knew a woman who'd get so wet in the cunt—like a load of mud. I sliced my cock at her and tore at her tits with my teeth until she moaned.

"'Oh, God,' she sighed. 'Put it in.'

"So I grabbed hold of it and rammed it up and up until it was fully buried. The minute it was inside she started twitching and jumping, tearing her nails on my shoulders, squeezing her legs around me. She jumped and heaved and poked herself up and down. I took her ass in my hands and rubbed away at the soft globes. I felt like I was going to shoot her cunt to pieces, and she wanted me to do it. I banged away, pounded, slid in and out. I wanted to bring the full length of my cock to bear on her incredible pussy, so I raised myself up and threw her legs over my shoulders. This tilted her cunt up and pulled my cock down so that my entire tool was drilling into her, up and down, up and down. Clara's eyes were glazed from the sensation; my cock filled every corner of her cavern and stretched her tight lips until I thought I would tear her. I drove into her with the mindless ferocity of an animal in heat, for such I truly was at that moment. I was mesmerized by my tool as it appeared and disappeared in Clara's ravenous slit. I grunted and moaned as I continued to drive into her; she was screaming at being penetrated so fully. When we both began to shake, I increased the pace until my prick was ravaging her mercilessly. My sperm exploded inside her with the force of a gunshot and coated the deepest recesses of her quim. At that moment, we leaped together into the air and rolled over and over in the grass, and we ended up with her on top of me.

"I had my eyes closed so I thought it was her shaking at me for more, and I can tell you I was ready for more. My pole was still hard. I poked it up and down a little. Then I looked up, feeling her get very heavy on me and I saw that the old guy had climbed on Clara and had rammed himself right up her ass. He was grinding away and biting at her shoulders, and she was bouncing up and down on me. I just lay there and let them take care of all the movements. It was lovely to feel the old man's balls slamming against mine and Clara's juice running down to my behind. He pounded against her while he reached around and crushed one of her enormous swaying breasts with his hand. I reached up and took the other, pinching the nipple and watching it lengthen until it stood out fully one inch from her mound. I kneaded the flesh back and forth, away from her other tit which was being manhandled by the old codger. The fingers of his other hand found her clit and teased it while my cock thrust placidly in and out directly below. I could hear his belly slapping against Clara's ass as he fucked her; his endurance surprised me. The way his spittle flew from his lips and his eyes bugged from his head, I felt sure his heart would fail before he could reach climax. Nevertheless, he succeeded in shooting an apparently copious amount of sperm into Clara's ass while I did the same in her pussy at nearly the identical moment.

"When we were done, the old man hopped off, and I pushed Clara away and stood up.

"'Listen, here,' I said to the man, 'what the hell do you think you're doing with my wife?'

"'Your wife, sir?' he asked.

"'Sure. I don't mind who puts it in her cunt, but her asshole happens to be my personal university. Who died and left you professor?'

"'But I had no idea—'

"'I'm not asking for ideas. I want to know where you think you get off—'

"'I assure you, I had no idea the lady was married.'

"'Married is not the point. What I'm talking about is her butthole. What were your *ideas* doing in there?'

"'There happened to be no signs forbidding the use of the cherished place, and since it was looking up at me with such an unoccupied expression, I thought the kindest thing would be to fill it.'

"'So you *thought*? So you had *ideas*! And what do you think your long pink cock is, a textbook?'

"'I'm terribly sorry about this—'

"'Sorry isn't going to do anyone any good. For that knowledge you've gained, I think it's only right that you pay your tuition.'

"'Do you mean...?'

"'Exactly. How many times have you entered the university?'

"Clara said, 'At least a dozen.'

"'That'll be a hundred francs a session—twelve hundred francs in all. And I hope this'll teach you a lesson.'

"'I don't have twelve hundred francs—'

"'How much *do* you have?' I asked, racing to his clothes before he could get there. In his wallet I found two thousand francs and some change. The old liar! I left him the change to get home with.

"'I think you'd better run along now,' I said to him.

"'I certainly intend to. I never realized Clara was involved in this kind of thievery.'

"'Thievery?' Clara asked.

"'What else would you call it?' the old man said.

"'Education,' she said.

"'In that case, you ought to pay me for having taught you a thing or two.'

"That got me interested. 'What did you teach her?'

"'I taught her the pleasures of love while standing on one's head.'

"'What a load that is!' I said, not believing him at all.

"'It's true,' Clara said.

"'So teach it to me.'

"'No!' said the old man. 'You'll probably take my change away under the pretext that you've taught me to do it while you watched.'

"'Go on and do it,' I said, 'or I'll tear your balls off.'

"What he did was, he picked Clara up, kicked all their clothes into a little pile beside a tree, and then turned Clara upside down, her head resting on the clothes, her body leaning against the tree. Then the old guy took a quick jump and landed on his head, and leaned his body against the tree. He and Clara wriggled their bodies up together and he pushed his cock into her twat. They couldn't do much jumping, but just swayed a little while he kept edging his rod in deeper. Their faces were red with the blood in their heads. They began to sway faster, both of them grunting like crazy. Clara's juice dripped along their bellies. His balls flopped wildly against his bottom, like two marbles rolling about. They jiggled away at it and after a few minutes, I could tell they were coming. They both sounded like pigs. Then suddenly, they came, and they both went flipping over in a dead faint to the ground.

"They came out of it in seconds.

"'I want to try it,' I said.

"'You'll have to wait a minute,' said Clara.

So I passed the time away by shoving my face into her cunt and slobbering away at it. Nothing like sucking a woman's cunt well-oiled with her own and a man's juice. A real meal of meat and wine. So I ate, and she went on panting with excitement. I licked all around her fragrant snatch, wetting the profusion of curly hair thoroughly. Then I concentrated more fully on the sensitive lips that I so loved to penetrate. I took the moist labia between my teeth and nibbled gently, first one side, then the other. I repeated the procedure when I found the swollen bud of her clit, taking the entire nub into my mouth and worrying it until Clara began to moan and squirm. At the same moment I dug my tongue against her slit and began to scour the inner membranes. My face was buried against her pussy and I dove into it deeply. Clara thrashed against me, murmuring how sensitive she was and how she wanted to feel my cock inside her again.

"'Now,' she said, 'I'm ready.'

"The old man turned her over against the tree, and then he helped me over and shoved me a little since I couldn't move. Clara reached up, took hold of my excited cock, and put the head into her cunt. Then we both pushed and it sank in to the bottom. The old man put my arms around her so I could play with her ass.

"I was getting dizzier by the second. My whole body was pounding like a pulse, like one enormous throbbing cock. We edged in and out, and I was feeling dizzy and sick, and at the same time more excited than I'd ever been. The rush of blood had made the head of my cock more than twice its usual size when erect. I felt as if my rod was swelling and swelling and would bust wide open. Her ass in my hands was like hot iron. We swayed slowly, and I was on the edge of fainting. And then, suddenly, at the moment I was coming, I went into a faint, my whole body heaved, and I shook and trembled. It was the greatest thing that ever happened to me. I came for what seemed an eternity, pumping thick spurts of sperm into Clara's grasping pussy.

"I didn't feel myself fall to the ground. I was just lost in the final moments of my orgasm which seemed to go on and on, like my whole body was oozing.

"When I woke up, the old man was gone. He'd pulled his clothes out from under us and had taken his money back. But I didn't care. It was certainly worth losing the money to have learned about this.

"'Are you all right?' I asked Clara.

"'Yes. Wasn't it wonderful?'

"'Great stuff.'

"'He's always having upside-down parties.

Everyone gets upside-down, all squeezed together, all fucking each other. It's really marvelous. But now, I suppose, he'll never want to see me again.'

"'So what? We'll have our own parties. Don't you like me better than him?'

"'Of course I do,' she said, and to prove it that mouth of hers started working away at my cock. I thought I wouldn't be able to get hard again after all our previous activity, but Clara's tongue was extremely persuasive. I was throbbing and bobbing erect as soon as she began lashing the head of my cock. By the time she covered me entirely with her mouth and clamped her lips over my shaft, I was like a bar of metal. My tool was burning hot and cold as she took me down her throat and began the suction that invariably drew the sperm from my balls. Only she wasn't content with that; she wanted to feel my enormity between her thighs. Ever eager to oblige, I turned her on her stomach, spread her legs, and entered her delicious pussy from behind. If anything, this position made her passage even tighter. Her walls gripped me almost suffocatingly as I slid in and out. Every inch of my cock was on fire as it snaked into her tunnel. She pushed back against me as I began a steady fucking motion. Little by little she assumed control until it wasn't even necessary for me to move; Clara simply thrust back against me and fucked me as I had fucked her so many times. She varied the motion and speed as she felt my cock swell—slowing down when it seemed as though I would come, speeding up so as to maintain the hardness of my shaft. Was there ever a woman like her? When she finally made up her mind to grant me release, she thrust against me hard until I spermed her uncontrollably. Then she got onto her knees and leaned against me, my prick still lodged inside her, while I fondled her tits and she became lost in the throes of orgasm.

"We fucked once more and then got dressed and left the wood. We took a taxi back to the bar in the center of Paris and drank and talked about old times. I told her I wished I didn't know her so I could rape her again.

"'I'm just in the mood for a rape,' I said.

"'Well, if you can't rape me, why don't you rape someone else? I'll help you.'

"'You will?'

"'Yes, but not just yet. I'd like to rest up a bit from our adventure in the woods.'

"'All right. Well, tell me what you've been doing all these years I haven't seen you.'

"She smiled. 'I've been fucking.'

"'All the time?'

"'All the nights, anyway. I've had some wonderful men.'

"'I'll bet they weren't as good as me.'

"'Oh, no, heavens!'

"'Tell me, Clara. Do you like my cock?'

"'Are you serious? You know I'm wild about it.'

"'Tell me more.'

"'What do you want me to say?' She reached under the table and dug her hands into my fly and began playing with my stiffening shaft. 'It's not the kind of thing you talk about. You use it. It uses you.'

"'I know, but tell me about it.'

"'It's tremendous. It's the longest one I've ever seen. Also the thickest. It's shaped perfectly. It's as hard as a diamond, as red as a flame. It shatters me and sears me.' She paused. 'Now, tell me about my cunt.'

"I reached up her dress and shoved three fingers right up her slit. 'That's what I want to tell you about it,' I said.

"'Is that all you have to say?'

"I dug another finger in, and she said, 'Now you're talking my language.'

"I said, 'Now tell me about my balls.'

"She let go of my cock and began to play around with my nuts 'I've told you,' she said.

"'No, no. Real words, I mean.'

"'You're conceited,' she said.

"'Conceited?' I said. Imagine anyone calling me that! 'Why, you cunt-faced little cocksucker!'

"'Never mind all this talk,' she said. 'I want some action. Let's go find someone for you to rape.'

"'Good idea. But I still don't like your calling me conceited. You be careful what you say or you'll be deprived of the best sausage any girl ever had.'

"So we went out and walked around for an hour or so, until we found a dark street. We strolled up the street until we found a door that was open and we walked through to see if the courtyard was a good place for rape. It turned out to be a little garden and Clara sat down on the ground.

"'A girl couldn't ask to be raped in a more comfortable place. I wish it was me you were raping.'

"'How can I rape you?' I asked her. 'You're the easiest fuck in Paris. And you know what I think?'

"'What?'

"'I think I didn't even rape you the first time. I think you raped me. That's how anxious for it you were.'

"She laughed and I squeezed her tits.

"'Push your cock in between them,' she said as she pulled off her blouse and bra.

"I did that, and she rolled her tits and got me so worked up I wanted to jump right on her. She seemed amused at the sight of my stiff rod between her generous mounds. She especially smiled when my red and swollen cockhead emerged just beneath her chin. Each time it did she lashed out with her tongue and left the knob glistening with her saliva. The sensation of my balls flopping against her chest, my shaft pumping between her breasts, and my cockhead being laved by her tongue drove me nearly insane. I was prepared to disregard our plans and simply throw Clara on the ground and drive my throbbing cock into her hot pussy. But she must have been aware of this, for she suddenly took my prick from between her tits and pulled away.

"'Well,' she said, 'you're in the perfect mood now for a rape.'

"We left the garden and stood at the door of the house waiting for someone to come by. But it was late and no one passed for a quarter of an hour.

"'Shit,' I said. 'I guess it's no use.'

"'Sh—' she whispered. 'Here comes someone now.'

"I looked up the street and saw a woman walking toward us. When she finally got up close, I turned to Clara and said, 'She's a whore. No use raping her.'

"The woman turned to us.

"'You don't have to rape me, honey,' the woman said.

"I saw she wasn't talking to me, but to Clara. She was a pretty good-looking woman, about forty, with a fleshy face and thick lips. She kept pushing her tongue out between her lips, licking them. She wore a thin blouse that was easy to see through even in the middle of the night and on a dark street. Under the blouse protruded a pair of thick tits that ended in big brown nipples. I reached out and, through the blouse, took one of the nipples between my fingers. It was as stiff as a cock.

"'My name's Marie, darling. What's yours?' she

murmured to Clara and rubbed her hand across Clara's chest.

"'My name is Clara,' she said. 'And this is Jean.'

"Then Marie pushed me away and backed Clara up against the door. They started kissing. Being left out of it, I fondled Marie's ass.

"I said, 'Let's go into the garden in back.'

"'That's a good idea,' said Clara.

"So we went back to the garden and stripped down. Marie was a real piece. I couldn't keep my hands off her hips and thighs and I was dying for a feel of her cunt. We all got down on the grass and formed a circle: Marie's cunt was shoved in my face; Clara's cunt was in Marie's face; and my cock was in Clara's mouth. Marie had a terrific pussy—as big as a sewer, and it ran like a faucet. You should have seen me licking it up. But she hardly even noticed because she was so busy working away at Clara. Her hands kept grabbing Clara's tits and pulling at them. My own hands were all over Marie; I loved digging my fingers into all that soft meat.

"Finally I decided I'd like to slip it into Marie, so I pulled my cock from Clara and I jumped on Marie who was still busy cunt-sucking. Her knees drew back and the big purple split stood up waiting for me. I obliged her and zoomed my rod right into her. Well, I have a long, thick one, but two like mine could've had room in Marie. Fortunately, I know how to take care even of such flabby cunts and I wriggled and shoved and she loved it. Meanwhile, Clara moved around so that, while she kept Marie's head between her legs, she could put her face right against my ass. And while I was pumping away, I felt her tongue licking in and out of my hole. It was a lovely treat. She reamed me well with that licker of hers. The tip of her tongue teased the ring of muscle around my anus, then began flicking in and out of the dark passage. Sometimes she varied the activity by biting my buttocks and nibbling at the bridge between my ass and balls. But she always returned to my rearward orifice, and gave it a cleaning I'll never forget. That's what I admired so much about Clara: nothing seemed to bother her. Nothing was beneath her. No degradation was beyond her. When she glued her face to my anus and began sucking at my hole I thought I would die. The effect of the entire episode was that my cock stiffened incredibly and my sperm began to jet into Marie's cunt. Not from the effect of Marie's flabby pussy, mind you, but from Clara's tongue blazing a trail into my asshole. And the moment I creamed up in Marie, Clara drove her tongue deep into my asshole and it was terrific.

"Afterwards we sat and talked and all the time Marie kept her hand in Clara's cunt.

"'I'm glad I met up with you two,' Marie said. 'I hope we'll have lots of pleasant meetings.'

"Clara took a little nibble at Marie's tit.

"'I tell you what,' I said. 'You girls can work for me, and then we can all be together very often.'

"'What kind of work?' asked Marie.

"'The same kind of work you've been doing all your life.'

"'And how much will I get for it?'

"'You'll get some good fucking out of me and some good fucking out of Clara.'

"'But a girl can't live on love, darling. How'll I pay my rent?'

"'You'll get one-third of every amount I get from a client you take on.'

"'How much will that be?' she asked suspiciously.

"'It depends on how much I think we can milk a client for.'

"'I don't know. I like a more definite arrangement.'

"'You stupid twat,' I said. 'You'll have twice as much business as you ever had. Who wants to fuck an old shit like you walking around in the streets?'

"'You did, for one.'

"'But I wouldn't pay for it. If you work for me, though, I get the money out of the client first, *then* bring him around to you. Then he has to like you, because he's already paid for it.'

"'Well...' She was considering it.

"'I'll work for you, Jean,' said Clara. 'And needless to say, I won't expect any money for it. Of course, I hope you'll see I get interesting types. I don't want someone who'll just shove it in, then leave.' She turned to Marie. 'You want to work for Jean, don't you, Marie?'

"'I don't know...'

"'Well, then, take your hand away from me until you do know.'

"'Oh, all right,' Marie said resignedly.

"Then the three of us all crawled together to seal the contract and, since it was dawn, Clara said we ought to call it a night.

"That's how Clara came to be one of my employees. She was a big success right from the beginning. She could take on five men in an hour and she could work steadily from midnight until dawn. I could ask really high prices for her. And she was pretty smart at getting more money out of her men than they'd paid to me before climbing on her. She'd say that for another hundred francs she'd show them something special, like putting her nipples up their ass. Her *piece de resistance*, of course, was the upside-down job and for that she'd ask for as much as two thousand francs at a time. And every franc she earned went right to me. She never took a franc for herself. I often felt guilty about it. Sometimes I'd say, 'You know, Clara, I wouldn't mind if you kept part of the money for yourself.'

"'Good heavens, Jean, I don't need the money. I love the work and I enjoy helping you out.'

"'You're an angel, that's what you are.'

"'And besides, all the payment I want is just a good fuck from you at least once a night.'

"She always got it. It was the very least I could do. Also one night every week would be devoted just to each other. Sometimes Marie would join us, but I liked to keep her out of it because when she was around I hardly ever got a chance at Clara's cunt.

"Well, this happy life went on for just about two years. My business grew tremendously during that time because the war had broken out and there were soldiers all over the place. Now and then Clara would take on three or four at a time and make a big happy family out of a bunch of foreign soldiers.

"I don't know how long our life together would have gone on if the Germans hadn't invaded. But then Clara got scared for her kid and she told me she was sorry but she was leaving Paris, going south.

"'You're crazy,' I said. 'There's probably a mint to be made out of the German army.'

"'Not through me, Jean. Don't you know the German army's all queer?'

"'Is that true?'

"'That's what I hear.'

"'Thanks for telling me. I guess I better get busy recruiting up an army of men for them.'

"The night before Clara left Paris we had a wild time together. We stood on our heads for about two hours and fucked, fucked, fucked. By the time she left I was so dizzy, I forgot to say goodbye.

"After that, for a whole week I went around Paris getting myself picked up by men and making them work for me. I was getting ready for the invasion, and by the time it came, I had eighteen men working for me.

"I never saw Clara after that. As a matter of fact, I often wondered what became of her. I thought maybe she was killed in the war, because otherwise, after the liberation, I was sure if she was alive she'd have come running back to me for more."

"Well," I said to Dupont, "she was alive, I'm sure of that."

"But how could she have gone on without me?"

"That I don't know. Maybe she found someone else."

"Someone else!" he said scornfully. "No one else could make her jump the way I did." You should have seen her when I had my cock in her pussy! She was uncontrollable."

"It seems, however, that she loved *me*."

"Love, love—who's talking about love? I'm talking about good, uncomplicated fucking." He looked at his watch. "It's late. I'll have to run along now. But say, maybe you'd like me to fix you up for the night—with my compliments. Any friend of Clara is a friend of mine. What do you go for?"

"Rose."

"Rose who?"

"The girl at the hotel where you used to live. She's the one who gave me your address."

"She's a good screw all right. Nice tits and still has a tight pussy. Go right ahead. Tell her it's on the house."

We shook hands and separated. I went back to the hotel where Rose was and climbed the steps to her room. The door was open again. I looked in and saw her lying on the bed, naked as before.

"My God," she said, "I thought you'd never come back."

"Your friend's gone?"

"Yes. Did you see Jean?"

I nodded.

"Any message for me?" she asked.

"Just that you're mine for the evening—with the compliments of the house."

"Get undressed," she said, rubbing the bush of hair on her loins. Her nipples were dark and erect. "I'm hot for you, honey."

I tore my clothes off and threw myself beside her on the bed. Pressing my throbbing cock against her belly, our mouths met, my hand stroking between her thighs.

"I can't wait," she said. "Fuck me quickly. Fuck me, you hot stud. I want you to sperm me until I can't take anymore."

With the instinct of a pigeon returning to its coop, my cock went gliding stiffly into Rose. She wanted to be fucked hard and fast, and that's what I gave her. I drove into her until the entire length of my cock was buried in her quim and my balls slapped her upturned buttocks. Without giving her a chance to settle herself, I began to pump into her furiously, squeezing her breasts and rolling her nipples between my fingers while I banged her. She began moaning and squirming almost at once, murmuring to me to ram my cock into her and make it come out her mouth. She was a wild one, and accepted the harsh screwing I gave her without complaint. What's more, she surely derived as much pleasure from it as I did, for her cunt became moist very quickly and each time I drove in and out there was a wet, squishy sound. There was nothing romantic or even passionate about it; it was simply raw sex. I realized that I was releasing my frustrations by fucking Rose this way...ridding myself of some of my anger for what Clara had done, and was doing to me. My cock pistoned relentlessly into Rose's willing sheath. As she began to scream that she was coming, my sperm rose in an irresistible torrent that swept into her pussy. I orgasmed in three great, mind-numbing gouts that left me drained of all strength and fury. I collapsed in a heap and lay senseless for a number of hours while Rose lay beside me. My mind was filled with visions of Clara.

CHAPTER
FIVE

V.

Less than twenty-four hours after my conversation with Jean Dupont, I was on an airplane bound for Nice. Since it was raining when we took off at Orly, the trip was not a pleasant one—the sky was thick with clouds, the plane bumped a great deal, and a good number of the passengers were sick. Past Lyons, however, the sky began to clear, and by the time we crossed the Maritime Alps, visibility was perfect. Villages appeared below, the bright sun beamed in the glass-blue sky, and in the distance the calm Mediterranean began to loom up.

We had perfect weather when we landed at Nice airport. I took a taxi to Cannes and checked in at the Hotel Superior, where I was given a splendid room facing the bay. It was only seven o'clock in the evening and the sun was still hot over the sea; a few bathers were out swimming or idling on the shore. Leaving my room, I had a drink at the bar downstairs and asked the attendant where I might find Rue de la Mer.

"It's a five minute walk from the hotel," he told me, and then gave me specific directions.

Rue de la Mer was not difficult to find. It was, like most of the streets in Cannes, very narrow and rather dark. As soon as I had emerged on the street, I once more examined Clara's list, found the house number and the name of the man. I continued walking to the end of the road and there found that the house corresponding to the number on my list was surrounded by a high stone wall. Well-kept double wooden doors were slightly ajar in the wall, and I pushed them open and stepped through into the front garden. The ground was cultivated; flowers of every color and variety grew thick around me. Going up to the front door, I pressed the buzzer.

Almost immediately, the door swung open and the butler looked out at me.

"Is this the home of Charles Bonnet?" I asked.

"Yes sir."

"May I speak with Monsieur Bonnet, please?"

"I shall have to see if Monsieur Bonnet is at home," he said rather snobbishly. "Who is calling, please?"

"Howard Cunningham, a friend of Clara."

He looked at me with suspicion. "Would you be good enough to wait a moment, please?"

He closed the door in my face. The butler's behavior annoyed me, but I couldn't deny the fact that his rudeness may have been justified, for seven-thirty in the evening is an odd time for an uninvited visitor to come calling.

After a moment, the butler returned. "Monsieur Bonnet will see you," he said.

I followed him into the house. He led me through several corridors and out to a sort of winter garden, which emerged upon the magnificent gardens in back of the house that had a view on the sea. A dozen people sat in a wide uneven circle, more or less around a long table covered with glasses, bottles, packages of cigarettes, and various appetizers. The atmosphere was one of luxury and laziness.

As I stepped out into the garden, one man stood up and came forward.

"Mr. Cunningham?" he asked.

"Yes."

"I'm Charles Bonnet. Please come and sit down."

I followed him to the table and he introduced me to his guests and to his wife, Louise, an angry-looking though attractive woman in her early thirties. Bonnet himself was older, possibly in his middle fifties; he was a wiry old man with grey hair and a grey moustache.

I sat down with him and his wife at a distance from the others.

"What will you take to drink?" he asked me.

I told him, and he went to bring me a glass. I was left alone with his wife. She seemed uninterested in speaking to me, but stared straight into my eyes. She was a most attractive woman: fair-haired with black eyes and golden skin. Her thin summer dress had buttons all the way down the front. The buttons were open along her chest and most of her very white breasts were exposed. In fact, when she breathed, little crescents of pink revealed themselves on either side and the breasts themselves seemed to become inflated. I wouldn't have minded sliding my cock between them and seeing just how tight a fit it was.

"Here you are," said Bonnet. He handed me my drink and seated himself opposite me.

I wondered how to open the conversation about Clara, particularly with Bonnet's wife sitting there, but this was momentarily postponed by Bonnet himself.

114

"Have you been in Cannes long, Mr. Cunning-ham?"

"No. I only arrived this evening."

"Ah, a real newcomer."

"Not exactly. I've been here several times before—although I've never actually stayed in the city."

"And you'll be staying here now?"

"Not for very long. A day or two, at most."

"That is very sad," said Louise Bonnet, and breathed so deeply I thought her nipples would pop out of her dress. "This is really the perfect time to be in Cannes—before the tourists and the very hot weather arrive."

"I know that," I said, "but it can't be helped."

There was a silence which was not so much awkward as tentative. It was the time to explain my purpose.

"I suppose," I began, "you must be wondering about the point of my visit."

"I confess myself guilty of a certain amount of curiosity, Mr. Cunningham," said Bonnet.

"Well—may I speak bluntly?" I asked, facing Louise.

"Of course," she said.

"The subject of my visit is rather a delicate one. Perhaps it may be wiser if I could see you, Monsieur Bonnet, alone for a few minutes."

Louise Bonnet looked at me coldly. "My husband has no secrets from me," she said.

"That is quite correct, Mr. Cunningham. Please feel free to speak openly."

I hesitated, took a sip at my drink, and began: "I've come at the request of Clara."

"Clara who?" asked Bonnet.

"It isn't likely you knew her by her own name. In any case, it was Clara Arvon."

Bonnet seemed to be reflecting seriously. He

looked off across the garden, his eyes resting on the darkening sea.

"I'm sorry," he said. "I can't recall having known anyone by that name."

"It's possible she used another name. She was a ravishingly beautiful woman with platinum-bluish hair, blue eyes—"

"Surely, Charles, you'd remember knowing a woman like that," Louise said to her husband.

"I imagine I would, but I'm afraid if I did know her I've completely forgotten her."

"She has sent you to see my husband?"

"In a way. You see, she's dead. She left a letter for me asking me to see several of her old friends. Monsieur Bonnet is one of the names she left me."

"Perhaps," said Bonnet, "there is another man in Cannes with the same name."

"She also left your address," I said.

"I see…" He paused thoughtfully. "How very odd. Were she and I supposed to have been good friends?"

"I haven't any idea. But the others on her list remembered her quite readily."

"Really, Charles," said Louise. "It's unlikely the woman would have bothered about someone she hardly knew."

"Yes, of course," he agreed. "But I honestly cannot recall her. I'm awfully sorry about this, Mr. Cunningham. I should have been very happy to help you—"

"It isn't terribly important. In any case, I'll be staying on in Cannes for another day or two, and if you should remember anything about her, you can reach me at the Hotel Superior. I hope you'll forgive me for having barged in on you this evening."

"Not at all," said Bonnet. "I'm delighted to have

met you. For those of us who live all year in Cannes, it's always a pleasure to see new faces before the season begins."

"Yes," said Louise. "Could you come here for lunch tomorrow?"

"I'd like very much to."

"Good," she said. "Come around noon. Lunch is always informal. If you go swimming in the morning, it's perfectly all right to come here in your trunks."

I shook hands with them both, aware of the warm pressure of Louise's fingers. Then, together, they showed me through the house and to the front door.

On the way back to my hotel, I tried to puzzle out the situation. Was this an additional twist of Clara's perversity? Had she planned this as a wild goose chase? It seemed likely, or at least possible, and yet I hadn't been convinced by Bonnet's denial. Well, I could try again at lunch the next day. I would have to plan my strategy carefully, try to insert something about Clara in the conversation that would elicit a response.

As it turned out, however, planning became unnecessary as soon as the desk clerk at the hotel gave me two telephone messages with my key. The first was from Bonnet:

Yes, of course, I remember Clara. I will meet you in the lobby of your hotel tonight at eleven and will tell you what you want to know.

The second message quite astonished me, for it was from Louise Bonnet. It said:

I will be waiting for you in the garden at two in the morning. I look forward to seeing you.
The desk clerk smiled as I read this note, and I

117

frowned at him and went up to my room. No sooner had I gone up than I realized how hungry I was. I washed, went downstairs, returned my key, and sought out a restaurant I had dined in years before. I ate a great deal, and ate very slowly, but still it was not quite ten o'clock when I went out to stroll along the promenade over the beach.

Here and there, below me, I heard the squeals and grunts of lovers mingling with the roar of the sea. And my thoughts were mingled with them—the story that Bonnet would tell me of his relations with Clara; Louise waiting in the gardens, her breasts bulging out of her dress, the pink flush of her nipples tautening under my kiss. Ultimately, in my thoughts at least, Louise was naked in the garden, and she waited for me to take her, to throw her onto a bed of flowers and join my flesh with hers. The image of our mating so excited me that I had to pause in my stroll in order to calm down. My prick was making a tent of the front of my trousers.

I leaned upon the railing and looked down at the beach. Below me, a boy and a girl—neither of them could have been more than eighteen—lay pressed against each other in wet bathing suits. The girl's suit had been pulled down beneath her breasts and the two ripening globes were as small and lovely as budding blossoms. One pink nipple was in the boy's mouth, and she stroked his back and sighed.

Suddenly he lifted his arms and began tugging at her bathing suit. It clung tightly to her body as he pulled roughly, passionately.

"Don't," she whimpered. "You're hurting me."

But he continued to pull the suit down her hips until her soft, gently swelling belly emerged. He put his lips to it and then pulled her suit down further, down to her thighs. The sparse triangle of hair appeared and he kissed it, then moved her bathing suit down her thighs, along her knees and calves, until the girl herself kicked it away. The boy's face disappeared between the girl's thighs; he had turned himself so that his covered loins were beside her mouth. Gently, she pulled his trunks down, and I heard her sigh as his penis jumped out at her, its thick head nudging at her lips. Her lips parted and she took the length of him into her mouth, her face buried in his pubic hair. I could see her tongue stroking his shaft, then moving up to lave his swollen cockhead. It flicked over the top before she throated him deeply again. They went on this way for several moments, licking, sucking, then they separated and turned so that their faces met and their bodies were pressed together. They kissed while his hand stroked between her legs.

"Let me," the boy said, moving his mouth from hers.

"I'm afraid. I've never done it before."

"There's nothing to be afraid of. Just relax."

"Will you stop if it hurts?"

"If you want me to."

On his knees, the boy moved between the girl's outspread legs. His cock bobbed eagerly in front of him; her pussy was a pink little smile in the shadows. Slowly, he raised her knees until they were folded back against her body, and the young, undamaged part of her was stretched and waiting. The boy moved forward, took his penis in his hand and guided its head to her slit. He slid it back and forth against her and the girl groaned with pleasure. The tip of his cock lay at the threshold of her sheath. He shoved gently, then out, and again a little more deeply, and pulled it away.

"Put it all in," the girl cried.

The boy lunged forward, dropping himself upon her, and his shaft ripped relentlessly into the girl. She gave one last gasp of agony.

"Take it out," she cried. "It's tearing at me. It hurts."

He worked at her for a few seconds until he knew the pain had given way to pleasure, and then he said: "Do you still want me to take it out?" His hips moved back and forth steadily.

"No, no," she whispered, grinding her body under him.

At that point, with belated discretion, I left the young people to their fun.

I returned to my hotel just before eleven and sat in the lobby until Bonnet arrived.

"You will forgive all this subterfuge," he said by way of greeting me. "I will explain it all presently. I have my car outside. We can drive over to a nice place I know outside the city. It would be more convenient to talk there."

I followed him out to his car, and no sooner had we climbed in then he drove off in the direction of Juan-les-Pins.

"The truth of the matter," he began rather breathlessly, "is that my wife is a very jealous woman and it was not until after our marriage that she learned of my somewhat outrageous past. Since she found this out, she has decided that for every woman I had before our marriage, she will have a man. Consequently, the virgin has turned harlot, and the lecher has turned saint. It is all a bit trying, so naturally I try not to let her know—or at least to keep her knowledge limited—of my activities in the years before our marriage."

"That's why you pretended not to remember Clara."

"Naturally. Needless to say, I remember her perfectly. And I also know exactly why you are here. She told me you'd come."

"She's dead, you know."

"So I understood from what you said before. I'm sorry to hear that."

"You haven't seen her in some time, I take it."

"Good heavens, no. Not since the war ended. Ours was, if you forgive the irony, a wartime romance. We met because of war; we separated because of peace. It was just as well; we felt little more than lust for each other, and were kept together by our common interests."

"Which were sex."

"To put it mildly. By the time I met Clara, ordinary sexual relations were a rather tedious appetizer for her. It was the variation that counted. She could go to bed with a dozen men, one after the other, or all at once, and still not find the thrill she was looking for."

"And what was the thrill?"

He shrugged. "When one is as debauched as she was, can there be any thrills left? Well, whatever sensations the body can experience, Clara experienced." He paused. "Ah, here we are. Just down the road."

He parked the car in the lot of a large building rather like a hunting lodge. We went around to the back where a large terrace with tables and chairs stretched down to the sea. There were a few people about. The place was lit by dim blue lights. Bonnet led me to a table at the extreme end of the terrace just a few yards from the sea. Here we were alone.

"Out there," said Bonnet, pointing seaward, "all through the war was a large yacht where Clara and I spent many evenings. We used to get a boat from this very terrace out to the yacht. It was an extraordinary vessel, but I'll tell you about it presently. First let's order something to drink."

We decided on a bottle of champagne. When it came, we toasted the memory of Clara, lit cigarettes, and I settled back in my chair preparing to hear Bonnet's tale. He took another sip of wine, and began:

"We met in 1943, in the very hottest days of summer. I enjoy swimming at night; I always have. What I like to do is to take my car and drive along the coast until I find a spot that pleases me. Then, I park at once, take my clothes off and go for a long swim in the warm sea.

"The night I met Clara, I had done just that. I had parked at a strip of lonely beach not far from here. I undressed, leaving my clothes in the car, and I went down the pebbled beach to the edge of the water. I remember still how warm the water was as I walked outward and began swimming. I swam for about a quarter of an hour before looking shoreward. When I did look back to the beach, I saw that I was roughly a hundred yards west of the place where I had parked my car. Since I was a bit breathless, I decided to begin swimming back at once, very slowly, so that I would not exhaust myself.

"But then, suddenly, I saw a woman standing on the beach. Naturally I couldn't, at that distance, see anything of her face or figure, but I could make out the strange movements of her arms which she held above her head as if offering herself to someone with the greatest abandon. She was alone, however. I was so curious that I made my way gently toward the shore.

"As I approached, I saw that she was naked. Her body was superb, covered with shadows, dark and sparkling; her breasts were full and tantalizing, and her nipples were ripe berries. She stood, as I said, with her arms raised and waving slightly—her round, succulent belly was thrust forward, writhing sensually. Moaning passionately, she lowered her arms and each of her hands began rubbing one of her nipples, stroking them until they grew stiff. She dropped one of her hands to her thighs and it inched its way to the mound of hair, then darted between her legs.

"Here, I thought, was a woman who needed a man!

"Pushing myself forward, I emerged upon the beach behind her. I walked toward her silently. When I was in back of her, I reached around and cupped my hands over her full breasts, pulling us so close together that my hot erection lay along the length of the cool split between her buttocks. She seemed not at all surprised, but pushed back at me and writhed her bottom. I dropped one of my hands from her breasts and led it across her cool belly and across the roundness of her thighs. Her thighs spread to admit my hand. Within, she was already moist: her hot juices oozed upon my hand.

"Abruptly she spun around and put her mouth to mine, her tongue digging between my teeth. I felt her pulling at me, and with one jerk both of us toppled over, Clara falling backwards to the sand with me on top of her. Our mouths remained together; I bit her lips hungrily and circled my tongue in the hollow of her cheeks.

"She moved her head aside: 'Bite me,' she said. 'Beat me.'

"I obeyed her, moving across each inch of her body, taking bits of flesh in my teeth and nibbling until I feared I might tear her apart.

"'Harder,' she'd cry.

"And my teeth sank deeper into her. Slowly, I cov-

123

ered her breasts, biting, nibbling—never too hard—until the pale globes were blue with small bruises. Then to her abdomen—a smooth, glowing swell of flesh. I covered her thighs and calves with bites, her buttocks, the small of her back, and at last prepared myself for the most delicious meal of all.

"Her legs went wider apart; her knees drew up and offered me the tangle of her loins. I sank my face against her womanhood and ate savagely, my teeth clamping upon a bit of fire-hot flesh and gnawing at it until she screamed. Brutish and impassioned, my hands clutched at the sand, pebbles, and broken shells around us, and taking masses of it I rubbed it on her body and into her loins, pushing it into her wet canal, and then underneath, forcing the debris into the tight passage of her anus.

"She was mad with desire and I threw myself upon her and pushed my cock through the web of roughness, inserting myself all the way into her. The sand burned my penis, giving it a sensation I had never before experienced. Clara screamed and shrieked and sighed in a mixture of agony and outrageous joy. Her legs locked me into her, and she heaved so that we began to roll, over and over, across the harsh, pebbly beach. Locked together in a searing embrace, we rolled without end, down the beach to the water. We spun into the water and were covered by the warm breakers.

"Then, when we were almost completely submerged, we stopped rolling. My hands grasped her breasts and pinched mercilessly, and I drove my member in and out of her, thumping wildly into the depths of her body, driving both of us to the ultimate precipice of pleasure. I'm sure it was a romantic scene, something right out of the cinema, but all I could think about was driving my cock as hard and as deep as I could into this fabulous woman. The waves splashed over us as I pumped my throbbing tool into her again and again, exulting in the way my entire body tingled with each stroke as her pussy clutched at me and seemed unwilling to ever let go. Our juices mingled with the liquids of the sea, and after the orgasm, we were so weakened that a wave sucked us apart.

"When I could get to my feet, I saw that she had managed to drag herself up the beach and was lying, panting, on a blanket I had not seen before. I went over to her, lay down upon the blanket, and we were silent for some time.

"At last she broke the silence. 'Thank you. That was marvelous.'

"'Don't mention it. It is my pleasure, I assure you.'

"'Do you live around here?' she asked me.

"'In Cannes. And you?'

"'I have a villa in the mountains. I drive down at nights to go swimming.'

"'And to have an adventure.'

"'Yes, but I rarely have one.'

"'I should think a woman like you would have men at her feet.'

"She laughed. 'Few men swim at night. And in such isolated spots.'

"'You always come to this same place?'

"'No. I usually go to different beaches. In fact, I've never been here before.'

"'But I hope you'll come back again.'

"'I certainly will—if you'll be here.'

"She reached across the blanket and took my already-restored penis in her warm hand.

"'How heavy it is,' she said.

"'That's because it's full.'

"'Full?'

"'Full of juice that must be emptied into you—to fill you with.'

"'I'm afraid,' she smiled, 'there isn't enough juice in the world to fill me with. I'm the container doomed always to be larger than the things I must contain.'

"'Not quite. I think I filled you quite nicely only a few moments ago.'

"'How long ago that was! So long, I can barely remember.'

"'Then I must prove it to you once more.'

"I edged myself close to her and took her in my arms.

"'I want to blow you,' she said, and slid herself around. Her puckered lips fit themselves over the head of my tool and the tip of her tongue flickered across my opening. Then her mouth moved slowly forward until my entire shaft was buried in the warm sheath of her throat. I moved my own face until it was lodged in the hair of her loins. Her flesh was smooth now, for the debris had been washed away by the water. I lapped at her lazily, my tongue trailing along her groove from her mound to her anus. I licked at the clitoris, then bit it, and she reciprocated by biting my penis. My tongue lay at the edge of her slit and I thrust it in and out like a snake, then pushed in as far as I could; I savored the hundred flavors of her wet interior.

"When we broke apart, she got on all fours and beckoned to me to get behind her. I did and I saw the gentle droop of her moist pussy lips. I led my instrument between them, pushing it to the twitching mouth of her vagina. I entered slowly, and she thrust herself back upon me until her buttocks were against my belly. We were once again sealed together. I reached round her, catching her breasts in my hands, and we started swaying, forward and backward. I slid one hand from her breasts to her crack, to the place where my rod was buried in her. With my fingertip I rubbed at her, just above the place of contact. I rubbed gently at first, then with increasing ferocity, and as the friction increased so did her passion until she was thumping backwards against me as though her loins must swallow all of me. I rubbed and she pushed until I felt our parts bursting upon each other, swollen with hot passion. At the moment of our climax, I reached both hands into her loins and tore at her clit like a madman. She screamed at the top of her lungs and pumped wildly back at me until our explosion ended.

"She sank down on her belly with me on top of her, and we lay breathing heavily for some time.

"'Would you like to go to a party?' I asked, climbing off her.

"'What kind of party?'

"'The kind you'd enjoy.'

"'I'd love to. Where is it?'

"'On a yacht out in the bay not far from Juan-les-Pins.'

"'Can I be back here by five in the morning?'

"'What's your hurry? It's after two now.'

"'I like to be at home for my little girl.'

"'Well, all right. We can be back at five if you like. The yacht's only about twenty minutes from the shore.'

"She dressed and we walked over to my car, where I put my things on.

"'My car isn't far from here,' she said.

"'Well, we can go in mine, and I'll drive you back here later on.'

"Perhaps I should explain now that all these luxuries cost an inordinate amount of money.

Gasoline—in fact, the whole operation of an automobile—was maintained by paying fantastic sums of money to the Germans. Even the maintenance of the yacht was upheld by consent of the occupying forces. For that reason there was no danger of having the law come down on that boatload of degeneracy. It was not until the war ended that the yacht's life came to a close.

"Well, Clara and I drove to this very terrace where several boats always waited to take members out to sea. I showed my membership card and paid for Clara's entry, then we climbed into the boat and were motored out to sea.

"'This is all very exciting,' said Clara.

"'Just wait until you get to the yacht.'

"'What happens there?'

"'Everything. Whatever you want you can have.'

"Clara sat close beside me, my arms around her, my hand fondling her breasts. A fresh salt breeze blew flecks of foam into our faces. It was not until we were a couple of minutes away from the yacht that its form became apparent to us.

"'It's certainly an enormous boat,' said Clara.

"'It used to belong to a wealthy Oriental prince. But he deserted it when the war broke out and it was taken over by a group of—what shall I call them?—sensualists. This group divided the boat into various sections in an attempt to accommodate people with even the most unlikely tastes. But here we are now, and in a moment you'll see it all for yourself.'

"A small elevator compartment had been lowered from the deck at the approach of our boat, and Clara and I climbed in and were pulled up.

"'Good evening, Monsieur Bonnet,' the attendant said.

"'Good evening. This is Mademoiselle Clara.'

"'I'm delighted to meet you. I hope you will find some entertainment to your taste,' he said.

"'I'm sure I will,' replied Clara.

"We went to the main door, through the lobby and into the cloakroom. As usual, two cloakroom attendants were at the desk—a young man and a young woman, both naked.

"'We leave our things here,' I told Clara, and we both proceeded to undress.

"Naked, we continued into the grand hall, a large nightclub affair where everyone from the musicians to the waiters was completely nude.

"'Oh, this is wonderful,' cried Clara.

"She stood for a while observing dancing couples, some of whom were dancing in the very midst of the love act. One man waltzed while the girl in his arms had her legs wound around him and their loins were linked together. In other parts of the hall, people ate, drank, talked, copulated, in fact did anything their hearts desired.

"'Would you like to dance?' I asked Clara.

"'Later perhaps. I'm so anxious to see the rest of the boat.'

"'Well, come out to the passageway.'

"I led her down to the lower deck. We stopped before a door from behind which came the most excruciating screams.

"'What goes on in there?' she asked.

"'Come in and see.'

"I pushed the door open, and no sooner had we crossed the threshold than we were attacked by a dozen people carrying sticks, whips, or other instruments. The large room was filled with people, some beating, others being beaten; couples lay together on couches or on the floor while men and women flogged them or trod on

129

them. Individuals were chained to the walls or hanging by their wrists or tied to posts set in the floor. And for every tortured person there was a torturer.

"'I rarely frequent this room,' I shouted to Clara, trying to push my assailants away.

"But I was lost to Clara. Passionate cries came from her as she yielded her body to the whips, writhing and turning so that no part of her would be left, as it were, undone. Her legs spread wide.

"'Here,' she shrieked. 'Here. Beat me here.'

"A monster of a man began lashing her and she screamed and rejoiced, until it seemed that steam rose from her cunt. The man threw himself upon her and drove his stupendous erection through her bruises and into her pussy. Others began to walk over them. He fucked her mercilessly, pounding away, his enormous cock driving in and out like a piston. All the while he crushed her tits with his hands and sucked her nipples.

"'Kill me, I'm coming,' Clara screamed, but at that moment the man withdrew his penis.

"'Don't stop,' she cried.

"He stood above her, delighted with her frustrated passion. But another man jumped down to replace the first, and although he was much inferior to the other, he nevertheless brought Clara quickly to her satisfaction with a few quick strokes.

"'Let's get out of here,' I shouted to her.

"'All right,' she gasped halfheartedly. I helped her to her feet and pulled her out of the room, slamming the door behind us.

"'Wasn't that fun!' she exclaimed.

"'Indeed, you seemed to enjoy yourself. But you're covered with bruises."

"'I don't mind. That's all part of the kick. What's all this?'

"We were passing a row of doors.

"'Oh, these are for people that want to be alone.'

"'No, that doesn't interest me just now. Let's go on to the parties.'

"We followed the passage to its end, but the next room was one to which Clara was not admitted—it was a room for men only.

"'Oh, I'd like to see that,' she said.

"'I'm sorry, but you can't. You could never pass as a man.'

"'I feel cheated.'

"'Well, if you come around to the passageway on the side, there's a concealed window and you can see what it's like inside.'

"'That's better than nothing,' she said.

"We edged into the passageway and with the help of two chairs we could see through the small window at the top of the wall. The room was flooded with men in every conceivable posture. In one corner, constructed like an altar, a gigantic stone phallus stood, and its worshippers were everywhere. Daisy chains extended all around the walls so that a perfect circle was formed: no bugger went unbuggered. The line swayed rhythmically, snakelike.

"'Isn't it marvelous,' said Clara, delighted.

"Whenever a man broke the chain, another was recruited from the center of the room to complete it.

"'The rumor is,' I explained to Clara, 'that the chain has never broken in the three years since it has come into existence. It goes on night and day, a replacement coming for every man who leaves.'

"Within the circle of the chain, dozens of men swarmed upon the floor; it was an endless panorama of cocks—cocks lunging into mouths or anuses. One man in the center of the room seemed particularly resourceful. He was on all fours and was surrounded by others; he held a penis in each of his hands, one in his mouth, one in his behind, and at the same time his own instrument occupied the rectum of the man beneath him.

"'How I envy him,' cried Clara.

"'Why?'

"'Well, I'd so much love to fuck and be fucked at the same time. But how impossible it is!'

"'You have certain other consolations for this failure.'

"'Such as?'

"'You can be fucked by two men at exactly the same time. And that is something no man can brag of.'

"'You think not?' she asked, pointing to the man in the center of the room who was now sandwiched between two others. Both his lovers were digging their members into exactly the same receptacle at exactly the same time.

"Disheartened, Clara climbed down from her chair and we continued on our journey.

"The next room was one to which I could not be admitted, for here women made love among themselves.

"'Good,' said Clara. 'That's for me.'

"She thrust open the door, there was sudden rush of thick flesh, and a sharp delicious smell of female wafted to my nostrils. Then the door slammed shut. I went around the side to the ventilating window, but three or four men were already crowded around it. 'Say, look at that beauty who just came in,' one man said.

"'She's the hottest one in the room,' said another.

"'Stop pushing,' said a third. 'I can't see.'

"'What a cunt on her,' said one and began thumping his poor prick with excitement.

"'Christ, this is too much for me.'

"'Me too. Let's get ourselves some live meat.'

"All the men—save the masturbating one—climbed down from their chairs and went off. Taking advantage of the vacancy, I jumped up and looked through the window. Truly, it was a paradise of women—fat ones and thin ones, short ones and tall ones, enormous-breasted ones and flat-chested ones, white ones and pink ones and black ones. There was every variety—from Clara the sublime to a hideous-faced, bony woman who raced around the room fondling breasts and buttocks, diving her face at every opportunity into dripping loins.

"'Oh, oh, oh,' moaned the man beside me, continuing to jerk off.

"Clara was being treated like a goddess. A group of worshippers led her across the room to an onyx bathtub. Powders and perfumes of such strong scent were poured into the water that the aroma drifted to my nose. Two women lifted Clara and laid her gently into the mass of bubbles in the tub.

"'I will bathe her,' a woman shrieked.

"'No, I.'

"'No, I.'

"'No, I.'

"A battle seemed inevitable. A dozen female faces turned red with jealousy and rage, and soon they were at each other. Arms and legs flailed, white teeth bit into fair flesh, long hair went flying, cunts were shredded by outraged fingernails, white breasts were colored with flecks of blood.

"'Stop this at once!' a voice commanded, and the women broke apart.

"A tall, beautifully-built woman approached them. Her bearing was aristocratic; her large breasts stood out grandly before her.

"'*I* will bathe her,' she said, and there was no more argument.

"This amazon-like creature knelt beside the bathtub and covered Clara's face with kisses. Then she climbed into the tub and with infinite tenderness began to wash every part of Clara's body. The amazon's foamy hands stroked Clara's bruised shoulders, then lovingly massaged her breasts, pulling at the nipples gently. Suddenly her hands disappeared beneath the water and the other women moaned at the thought of the treasure their leader was exploring. Clara leaned her head back, a smile on her lips, and she gave herself up to the amazon's manipulations.

"The man beside me was groaning heavily and I looked at him in time to see a tremendous jet of cream spurt from his tool to the wall; he throbbed with his orgasm. When the wall was coated with his juice, he said, 'That's the twelfth time I've done it in two days.'

"'Really?'

"'Yes. Eight times yesterday. Four times today...so far, that is.'

"'Masturbating?'

"'Yes.'

"'Why do you do it?'

"He shivered and shrugged. 'Because I love to.' And he was once again pulling on his penis, bringing it to its full length. He fisted it roughly, his eyes popping from his head.

"When I turned back to the lesbian chamber I saw that Clara was now washing her bath-companion. Another woman approached the tub carrying a thick Turkish towel and Clara stepped out of the tub to be enfolded in the towel and the woman's arms. Each part of her body was patted in turn and when she stood naked her skin fairly glowed.

"A comb was brought by a plump old lady who

proceeded to comb Clara's gorgeous hair until it hung soft and loose to her shoulders. Then the old woman knelt and combed the hair of Clara's loins, running it across her mount and smoothing the thick mass of curl.

"After this, a pot of oil was brought and Clara's body was coated until it seemed magically golden. Her beauty was unearthly. All activity had ceased in the room and she was surrounded by admirers. A thousand loving hands reached out to touch her; lips were pressed to her oily flesh. At this point, the amazon, who had disappeared for several moments, returned. Strapped to her belly was a black rubber dildo, its proportions would have put any man to shame. At that instant, I actually feared for Clara's safety—although, in truth, she seemed singularly unperturbed by it.

"She was lowered to the floor and at once two women came to her. The first sat on her face, thrusting her purple pussy lips to Clara's mouth. The second squirmed between Clara's thighs and did to Clara what Clara did to the other. A dozen more women surrounded her, their tongues flicking across her body.

"Suddenly Clara was let alone. Two girls appeared and each took hold of one of Clara's round buttocks. They lifted her until her slit was wide and tantalizing with oils and her own juices. Her knees bent back; the amazon closed in and drove the dildo into Clara's cunt. The lovers writhed ecstatically. Women crawled under them and over them fondling and licking any unoccupied space.

"It was an incredible sight—Clara's body covered with the squirming bodies while the huge dildo rummaged in her cunt. A dozen mouths roved over her breasts, nibbling the engorged nipples, licking her belly and hips in an orgiastic frenzy. The amazon continued her steady motion, driving forward and down, fucking Clara as though the cock were a real one attached to the heated loins of a man. Clara's pussy grasped at the rubber organ, her flesh extending as it was pulled from her. She seemed in a trance; her eyes saw nothing as her body accepted the homage of the crazed women.

"Clara trembled as the rubber cock dug in and out of her. I could hear her sobs of joy. Beside me, the masturbating man was rapidly approaching his thirteenth climax. Everyone seemed on the verge of madness. The chamber of women literally throbbed with orgasmic excitement; piles of female flesh rose as the lesbians heaped upon each other. My own passion came to such a pitch that I thought I must imitate my companion or die. I pulled at myself wildly and my chair shook; screams rose from everywhere; my heated rod was at the bursting point. And then, at that moment, there was a universal climax. Clara screamed with her orgasm; the others joined with her. Simultaneously, I and the man beside me unloaded a torrent upon the wall.

"When I had recovered, I saw Clara lying impotent upon the floor of the room. The dildo was now being strapped to her loins. Obviously she was to repay the amazon for the latter's kindness. What I saw this time, however, was that the dildo was a double-edged weapon; one end was plunged into Clara and the other into the amazon's pussy. The orgiastic rites were repeated, with everyone but myself participating as before. Even the man beside me, though with some difficulty, was working himself toward another orgasm.

"Soon afterwards, Clara emerged.

"'Did you see?' she asked me.

"'I certainly did.'

"'I was treated like a queen.'

"'And a king.'

"'That is a room I will often go to.'

"She looked around suddenly and saw the masturbating man.

"'What's he doing?' she asked me.

"'I think it's quite obvious.'

"She approached him thoughtfully. 'Why don't you find a partner?' she asked.

"'I don't want one.'

"'Why not?'

"'Because I like to jerk off.'

"She looked at his penis a while and said, 'Let me touch it.'

"'No.' He turned away from her.

"'Please. It's a beautiful one. Long and thin. Wouldn't you like me to suck it a little?'

"'No.'

"Reaching forward abruptly, she tried to grab hold of his inflamed member.

"'Let him alone,' I said to her.

"'But I want him,' she said passionately.

"'Here, you can play with mine,' I suggested.

"'I'll play with yours later. Right now, I want to play with his.'

"'No, you can't,' he told her firmly.

"Enraged by her frustration, she screamed at the man and I had to drag her away.

"'Calm down,' I said. 'There are still many rooms to be seen.'

"'I don't want to see anything else,' she pouted.

"'Don't be such a child. Simply because a man refuses to let—'

"'He's the first person who ever said no to me.'

"'Well, you can't expect to have a raving success with everyone. Come along now—'

137

"'No, I want to go home.'

"'You're ridiculous.'

"'I must go home. I'm probably late already.'

"'All right. I'll take you back to your car.'

"We returned along the way we had come, following the passageways and going up and down various decks. At last we emerged once more in the grand ballroom. There were still a few people dancing, but they were dancing to phonograph records since the men in the band had come down to find themselves women. What went on here, at this point, was a huge melange of all that had been going on in the other rooms.

"'One dance,' I said to Clara.

"'No, it's really too late.'

"'You promised.'

"'Honestly—'

"'You did say you would.'

"'Well, all right. Just one.'

"And so we came together and moved across the floor. Her body was still oiled and my awakening prick slid across her belly. Dropping my hands from her back to her buttocks, I squeezed her tight against me and felt her slippery flesh rub against mine. My fingers edged in between her buttocks and skidded with oily ease into her anus. Leaping up, she wound her legs behind me. Her hand found my cock and she forced it down, shoving it between the thick greased hills. It rode easily into her pussy. Our mouths met, tongues sucking together, and she writhed and squirmed, urging the pressure of her body upon our connection, making it tight and maddeningly exciting. I ground my hips, pounding against her, faster, ever faster, and her teeth bit hard on my lips. The succulent greased sound of our thumping loins drowned out the phonograph music. It thrilled me to look down and see my rock-hard lance plunging in and out of her. Holding each other, we banged together wildly and brought each other to our pleasure.

"Afterwards I refused to release her and in this position we went to the cloakroom to get our things. My tool remained in her box. By the time we got there, our movements had again excited us and we started grinding once more. The young man who attended in the cloakroom came out from behind the rack and approached us. He stood in back of Clara, edged forward and drove his penis into her oily behind. He began slamming against her, his balls flopping back and forth with each stroke. The three of us danced around the room in a frenzy while the attendant and I bucked away at Clara from both ends. We pounded her breathless and would not release her until, front and back, she dripped our liquid.

"We dressed hurriedly and took the boat back to the shore. I drove her back to our place of meeting where she climbed into her own car and rode off.

"There was no need to make an appointment, of course. From then on we knew where we might find each other. And, indeed, until after the war ended, I doubt that Clara ever missed one evening on that yacht. Needless to say, there were times I wouldn't see her for weeks on end. Not having her endurance, I'd have to take a month's vacation from the yacht now and again. And sometimes Clara would be occupied with others. But, generally speaking, we were as much lovers as any people are who live that kind of life.

"We continued in exactly that way until the war ended. All the members of the yacht knew that our club would be closed down, and we had a terrific party the last night. Twenty virgin girls and twenty virgin boys were introduced to the pleasures of passion in all its manifestations. The daisy chain, hitherto unbroken, was joined by every man on the boat before its long and arduous career came to an end. And most delicious of all for Clara, the man who had stood masturbating outside the lesbian chamber allowed her not only to touch his penis, but to pump him to an orgasm.

"So our party ended. And Clara went back to wherever she had come from. I confess I was not sorry to see her go. Soon afterwards I vowed I would change my ways and married the young woman you met this evening. Our marriage has been one of extreme happiness—interrupted only when tales of my former life come to Louise's ears."

Bonnet, having finished his story, drained our third bottle of champagne.

"Good heavens, I'm tired," he said.

"There was quite a bit to say." I looked at my watch. It was a few minutes after two. "I really must be going."

"I'll drop you off."

"Are you going home?" I asked.

"No, of course not. How can I? And I *am* beastly tired."

I was silent with embarrassment. No, I decided, I wouldn't deceive this very nice man. I would go straight home to bed.

"Listen," he said to me, "if you're thinking that perhaps after all you won't go and have some fun with my wife—"

"But how did you know about that?" I cried, incredulous.

"I've lived with the woman seven years. Now,

look here, you'll be doing me a favor by going over to her. If you don't, she'll find someone else. And frankly, I'd much prefer she took you on."

"That's very kind of you—"

"Nonsense. One has got to come to terms with the world, hasn't one?"

"I suppose so."

"Well, come along. I'll drop you at the house."

We drove back to Cannes in silence. I was thinking how strange it was that Clara's attempt at revenge had backfired. The more I learned of her life after we separated, the more distant she seemed. That evening I was more concerned with Louise Bonnet than with the memory of Clara.

When we were not far from his home, Bonnet said, "You will be a good fellow, won't you?" he asked.

"What would you like?"

"First of all, will you not forget to use these?" And from his pocket he took a package of rubber contraceptives. "There are a dozen of them."

"It's hardly likely I'll need all of them."

"One never knows," he laughed. "In any case, you must promise to use them. As much as I am fond of you, I should really dislike having to be the father of your child."

"I understand," I agreed. "I'll use them."

"Secondly," he continued, "I'm dead tired, so try not to stay on forever. And last of all, don't forget about lunch tomorrow."

"Indeed I won't."

He stopped a few yards before the house. "Here you are."

We shook hands.

"Good night," I said.

"Good night. And have fun."

He drove away, and I went down the street to his home. The doors were open and I walked through into the front-garden. Since Louise wasn't there, I followed the path around to the back of the house. The garden here was even more splendid by moonlight than it had been at sundown. I looked around but couldn't not see her. All the lights were off in the house. I thought that perhaps she had decided I wasn't coming and had gone to bed.

I wandered round the garden, picked a sprig of mimosa from a tree, and considered returning to my hotel.

"Are you looking for someone, Mr. Cunningham?" I heard her voice from behind a cluster of trees at what I had thought was the end of the garden. I walked toward the trees and found that the garden continued for some way. There, in the midst of the trees, flooded with moonlight, was Louise Bonnet. She was not, as I had imagined in my reverie earlier in the evening, naked. In fact, she wore the dress she had worn before, and it was even buttoned a bit higher. She looked ravishing in the moonlight.

"Yes," I said. "I was looking for you."

"For me?" She seemed incredulous. "For me? Why, what an extraordinary hour to come calling. It's a good thing my husband's out or—"

"What are you talking about?" I said breathlessly. "I got your telephone message at my hotel and—"

"Telephone message? I left no message for you."

There was something so utterly frozen in her voice that I felt momentarily convinced a trick had been played on me.

"Obviously, there's some mistake," I said.

"Obviously."

"Then I'll say good night."

"Good morning would be more accurate."

"Good night then, and good morning."

I turned around to leave, but stopped myself, and turned back to her. Moving rapidly, I crossed the ground between us, grabbed her into my arms and forced my lips against hers. She tried to push me away. At first I resisted her efforts, but at last gave way.

"You're a maniac," she said, but this time I knew that this was all part of a game. Louise Bonnet was playing this thing out with the hope I would rape her.

"Come here," I shouted, and pulled her toward me, thrusting our mouths together again. My tongue groped between her lips, forcing her teeth apart. All the time she fought and scratched; I would not relinquish my hold.

When I released her I held the neck of her dress in my hands and pulled in either direction so that all the tiny buttons burst along the length of her dress and bounced to the ground. Beneath, she was naked. I tore the garment from her body and stepped back to look at her. She covered herself with her arms, trying to hide her nakedness, but little was hidden. The two luscious mounds glared out at me, their nipples stiff and purple in the moonlight. Her bush was a darker shadow in this place of shadows. Taking her arms, I threw her to the ground.

"Don't move," I said, "or I'll kill you. I'm going to fuck you good."

She lay quietly in mock terror as I stripped myself. Her eyes widened at the sight of my cock as it sprang free. When I flung myself upon her she once more pretended to be fighting me off. When I reached between her thighs, she squirmed so intensely I could not take hold of her, but my hand felt the dripping moisture of her passion. I forced her thighs back and she turned and jumped, and when I aimed my cock at her slit, she moved violently to prevent entry. I drove forward and missed because she turned. I thrust again and the tip of my member penetrated but was thrust away when she made a rapid movement. I tried once more and this time hit center, sinking deep into her flesh. My balls slapped her upturned buttocks as I began to pound into her. She continued to wriggle and shake, but now her legs kept me bound to her.

I began pumping into her while I crushed her tits with my sweaty hands. This was, after all, what she wanted, and I don't say this from the warped perspective of the rapist. As I fucked her and let her pleas and protests fall on deaf ears, she continued to pull me to her so that my cock sank more deeply into her hungry pussy. She was thrusting up against me, driving my lance into her flesh, while she told me what a filthy animal I was. Well, if that was how she liked it, I was more than willing to make real her fantasy. I twisted her nipples and rolled my hips, drilling her fiercely. She groaned and made a feeble protest that changed to a coo of pleasure as I screwed faster and faster. My cock plunged in and out, stretching her taut little slit and exploring her moist tunnel. When I felt my sperm rising I reached under and slid my hands beneath her buttocks, raising them up and opening her quim to me even more. My tool ravaged her until she began to scream breathlessly and flood me with her juice of passion.

Afterward, when we had broken apart, she pretended to be outraged. "How dare you do a thing like that!" she cried.

"I'm desperate," I said. "Besides, you were a great fuck."

"You know I can tell the police and have you arrested at once."

"I'd kill you if you did."

"I believe you would. You're a filthy brute."

She drew herself to her feet.

"Where do you think you're going?" I asked.

"Into my house."

"No, you're not. I'm not done with you yet."

"You monster," she shrieked as I pulled her to the ground once again.

"Shut up. I don't want any noise out of you."

I rolled over so that I was on my back and she was above me. I held her by the hips and raised her so that she hovered over my erect prick. Then, when my cock was centered, I simply released her weight and let her fall upon my shaft. Her eyes rolled up in her head as I impaled her with the full length of my lance. Her bottom came to rest on my belly and I pulled her forward. I began to thrust up and into her until she picked up the motion and rocked upon me without my urging. The sensation was exquisite as she thrust her pelvis forward and back, milking my cock with her tight pussy. She had little to say at this point, simply closed her eyes and continued to fuck herself on my pole. I reached up and cupped her breasts, massaging the pendulous flesh until her nipples stood out thick and dark. Then I began to force myself more harshly into her quim, increasing the pace and driving my cock in and out to its full length. The flush of passion rose from her belly to her neck as she moaned gutturally and flooded my joystick with her cream. I shot my load into her eager pussy immediately thereafter.

Needless to say, this whole game brought me close to laughter. Yet, in some perverse way I enjoyed it as much as she. I raped her twice more that evening, and then went back to my hotel. I slept until eleven, went down to the beach for a swim, and then walked over to the Bonnet house for lunch.

It was a pleasant lunch with several other people present. Bonnet was charming and disappeared as soon as the meal was over. I was rather amused with the difficulty Louise had in getting rid of the other guests. Finally, when everyone had gone but the two of us, she addressed her first words of the afternoon to me.

"I haven't said anything to my husband about last night. I suggest you leave now and never come back to this house."

"Not just yet," I said.

"I hope you aren't expecting a repetition of last night's outrage!"

"Exactly!"

And, rising from my chair, I picked her up in my arms and carried her into the cluster of trees. I lifted her skirt and brutally tore the panties from her. Her pussy was already wet, I noticed with some satisfaction. Drops of moisture bedewed the attractive moss on her mount. I lowered my head and lapped them from her while she writhed in my grasp.

"Now then, would you like me to fuck you as I did last night?" I asked mockingly as I pulled my throbbing weapon from my trousers.

"No, you bastard!" she gritted as I moved between her thighs. "Let me be. Don't you dare."

"Just as I thought. You *do* want it." I thrust forward and drove my cock into her pouting slit. "And now you're going to get it."

"No, no," she moaned, but she raised her legs of her own accord and stretched her slit even wider for my rampaging tool. "No. Don't. Stop. Don't…stop. Don't stop. Please…"

I smiled grimly. This one knew what she wanted

and how she wanted it. I drilled into her again and again, letting her have the full benefit of my length and girth. I pulled back until only my cockhead was just inside her delicious folds, then plunged forward repeatedly. She quivered and shook as she came in a rush, feeling at the same time my hot sperm burning a path into her house of joy.

I took the evening plane back to Paris, musing the trip away with my memories of Cannes. Strangely enough, it was not until we landed at Orly that I reached into my pocket and found the full, unused package of contraceptives that Bonnet had given me the night before.

CHAPTER
SIX

VI.

Having returned from Cannes, I made my inventory: I had covered half of Clara's list—and in doing so, had committed adultery, had an evening (gratis) with a whore, posed for nude photographs, and heard a number of strange tales and encountered several very curious people. I could scarcely believe my behavior. This situation in which I found myself seemed to induce in me the most atypical responses…at least insofar as my customary behavior was concerned. Yet, I felt the need to see the affair through to its end. Half the list was done, and yet three more visits remained to be made, as well as a trip to a village near the Spanish border.

The fourth name was Rex Baxter—obviously an American or an Englishman. I rang him up the morning after I returned to Paris.

"Hello," he said in a pleasantly crisp British voice.

"Mr. Baxter?"

"That's right."

"My name is Cunningham…Howard Cunningham. I'm an old friend of Clara's—"

"CLARA! Good heavens! I was just reading about her in the newspapers the other day."

"Awful, isn't it?"

"Hideous. Who did you say you were?"

"Howard Cunningham."

He hummed across the wire an instant. "I say, I've heard that name before."

"From Clara. I'm an old boyfriend of hers."

"Oh, of course. That's it. You threw her over—or something like that."

"In a way. Look here, do you think I might come over and see you for an hour or so?"

"Certainly. Delighted. Can you come along right now?"

"Yes, I can."

"Good. Do you have the address?"

"Yes, Clara left it for me."

"Then I'll be expecting you."

I walked to Baxter's place. His apartment was in a house that overlooked the Tuileries. Baxter himself answered my ring.

"Come right in," he said.

He was a short, slight, blond man with rather feminine features. He could have been a well-preserved fifty or an ill-used twenty-five; actually I thought he was not more than thirty—there was a certain awkwardness in his manner that had not yet been rubbed away by experience.

Leading me into the enormous, sunny salon which looked down upon the famous gardens, he said, "You know, I do remember Clara having said something about your coming to visit me one day. But I thought surely it would never happen. Please sit down. What will you drink?"

"I really don't—"

"How about some nice tomato juice—in token of

the morning...spiked with vodka...in token of the sunshine."

"All right," I said.

He left the room and returned after a moment with two glasses filled with dazzling red liquid.

"Blood and spirit. To Clara's inevitable end," he toasted. "Forgive my indelicacy."

We drank.

"Now," he said, drawing his chair up beside mine, "tell me what I can do for you."

"Well, Clara left me a letter, listing your name among others. Her request was that you tell me of your relationship with her."

"Yes?"

"That's all. The rest is up to you. If you're willing—"

"Of course I'm willing." He paused. "The only thing is that it is such an odd tale..."

"After the other stories I've heard of Clara's adventures, nothing could shock me."

"Perhaps not. But I'm not quite sure. In any case, I'll tell you all there is to tell, but you must assure me that if you're shocked, you'll stop me. I simply couldn't go on talking to a horrified audience."

"Yes. I agree. In the eventuality that I'm shocked, I'll stop you."

And so, for the fourth time, I settled back with a drink in my hand to hear a tale of Clara's lust:

"First of all, Mr. Cunningham, I must give you some idea of myself. I am an individual for whom love is indivisible: that is to say, for me sex is equally agreeable whether with a woman, a man, a beast—or even objects. Everything on earth has a certain irresistible appeal for me. I will exclude nothing or no one from my bed. I've always been this way: Nature, as you may know, shapes the libertine in childhood.

My first memories of sex, in fact, go back to my mother's death—or immediately afterward, when my drunken father brutally raped me one night and many nights thereafter. When he remarried, his new wife took me as husband in the afternoons. I was made to fuck her day after day...a not-unpleasant experience for a young man I should point out. At school, I was corrupted by—or, to tell the truth, I corrupted—teachers and students alike. I was, and am, insatiable. What is more, I create insatiability in many people I meet.

"After the war I came to Paris, a student of little means. Some of my money came from admirers, for even the French took a certain interest in me. Shall I describe all my degenerate ways to you? Let me give you one example, one that goes back to 1947.

"I had fallen in with a rather wealthy group of people. The richest of them all was a woman named Marcelle. One day she told me that she was planning a costume ball at her home in the country. Would I come? she asked. Needless to say, I was delighted. Having little money of my own, I set to work putting together a costume for myself. I had chosen to go as Cinderella, and I worked a good many hours on the gown and on a wig of white wool. By the time the day of the ball arrived, I was ready to appear as a most ravishing Cinderella.

"Being short, and having small features, I knew I would be able to deceive strangers into thinking I was a woman. But I wanted also to deceive those I did know. To do this required a feat of makeup, and I labored lengthily over this, putting layers of powder upon my face and wearing color on my eyes. The result, extraordinary as it may seem, was a perfect woman. My bodice was filled out with two false rubber breasts whose shape and texture was so uncanny that, after taking on my body's warmth, even I was deceived by them.

"Masked, I arrived at Marcelle's home, and in fact no one did recognize me. Those whom I knew looked at me curiously, then turned to one another and asked who I could be. I danced with men and women alike, and I deceived everyone. How splendid it is to be at once known and unknown, to be both man and woman. Needless to say, I was so taken with myself that I paid very little attention to others.

"Actually, I paid little attention until just before midnight—at which time the most extraordinary man appeared in the ballroom. He was dressed as Robin Hood, masked and bearded. The tights he wore were so revealing that everyone's eyes were glued to the outline of the man's genitals. I confess that I was overwhelmed. Taking advantage of the situation, I walked over to him, wondering how far I dared go without giving myself away.

"'Good evening, Robin Hood,' I said to him.

"'Good evening, Cinderella.' He bowed to me and I bowed back.

"'I am sure I know who you are,' I whispered, not having any idea, but in order to keep the conversation going.

"'Who am I ?'

"'You are—you're Jules de Marville.'

"He laughed; it was a soft, musical laugh. 'No, I'm not de Marville. And all the Jules are in your eyes.'

"'Robin Hood can really flatter,' I said rather nervously.

"'I never flatter. It's quite true. But you haven't guessed who I am.'

"'Well, if you're not de Marville, I can't imagine who you are.'

"'Then, shall we make a deal?'

"'Perhaps…'

"'I'll trade my name for yours.'

"'Oh, no,' I said. 'That's no trade. I'm Cinderella and no one else.'

"'In that case, Cinderella, will you dance with one who is neither Marville nor Robin Hood?'

"We walked to the center of the floor and he put his arms around me, drawing me close to him. Almost the moment we were together I was amazed to sense the pressure of his rock-hard tool against me. What an irresistible woman I had turned out to be! My difficulty was, however, that, while dancing, my own penis had begun to stiffen, and I feared that, should he feel it, I might end the evening with nothing more romantic than a black eye.

"'Let's go out into the garden,' I said, interrupting the dance.

"'I should love to.'

"We walked with his arm around me. Since there were many couples in the area immediately around the house, we strolled for five or six minutes before sitting down on a rough wooden bench in a concealed part of the garden.

"'What a wonderful night it is,' he said, his arm dropping from my shoulder to my waist.

"'Yes, it is,' I agreed, rather breathlessly. I knew we would not spend the rest of the evening discussing the weather, and I wondered what I might do when his embraces would begin threatening to give my secret away. What would I do if he tugged at my breasts and found them removable? What would I do if he longed to touch a woman's soft places and found instead something as hard as the instrument that even now bulged from his loins?

"Without thinking, madly attracted to the very

bulge I've mentioned, I reached out and put my hand over his tights. The length and thickness of his cock dazzled me, and I realized what I had done and pulled my hand away.

"'No,' he said. 'Don't stop.'

"'I mustn't,' I said.

"'Why mustn't you, for heaven's sake?'

"I shook my head. 'I can't explain. I simply mustn't. Believe me.'

"His arms went around me in a powerful grasp, and he pulled my face to his, bringing our mouths together. I tried to keep my mouth closed to his insistent tongue, but its sweetness coaxed my lips, and at last I relented, relaxed the drawbridge of my teeth, and allowed him into the castle of my mouth. Our tongues met and lapped at each other until I was blind with passion. Suddenly I felt his hand moving along my neck, descending along my chest. In a moment, it would grope into my bodice.

"I'm lost, I thought. Lost.

"Terrified, I wanted to break away, but passion refused to allow me, and I gave myself recklessly to the kiss, pushing inevitability out of my mind.

"With calm certainty, his hand dug down my dress and took the firm, warm, rubber breast in his hand. He didn't seem to notice anything unusual, and with relief, I threw caution to the winds and let my hand stray once again to the tremendous lump in his tights.

"After a moment, his hand released my breast and soon reappeared at my ankle. It strayed upward, sliding over calf and knee, and then gently, with infinite tenderness, stroked my thigh. I snapped my legs together with violent determination.

"'What is it?' he asked.

"'You mustn't touch me there.'

"'Why not? I want to.'

"'No, please.'

"'Surely there must be some explanation. I know you desire me.'

"'Yes, I do, but—'

"'But what? Tell me.'

"And then I had an incredibly brilliant idea. 'You can't,' I said. 'Because—'

"'Because why?'

"'It embarrasses me to say it.'

"'Nonsense. You mustn't feel embarrassed with me. Please tell me.'

"Lovingly, coaxingly, he planted little moist kisses along my neck. 'Tell me,' he said.

"'Well, the truth is—I'm having my period.'

"He burst into laughter. 'Do you think a little blood will frighten me?'

"'It's not only you—but I myself can't bear to be touched there at these times.'

"'Let me, and I'll show you the pleasures of it.'

"'No, no.' And then, gathering my courage, I made the recommendation I had been longing to make from the moment I saw him. 'But there are other ways.'

"'Other ways?'

"'Yes, other passageways through which your passion may travel.'

"He smiled. 'I understand.'

"We were silent as I stood up and knelt before the bench, leaning my elbows on the rough wood. He knelt behind me and I felt him lift my gown. Gently, he lowered the panties I wore and pressed his warm lips upon my buttocks. Then he paused and I trembled at the sound of his own clothing being lowered.

"His hands went again to my flesh and drew my buttocks wide. His fingers probed my asshole, stretching the taut ring of muscle. I felt the enormous head of his penis touch my delicate flesh. He thrust, once and again, ripping me, and inserting his length into me. Bound together, we remained motionless. Then his arms went round me to fondle my breasts. But only one hand stayed at my breasts; the other descended, descended, descended.

"So taken was I with my role of woman that I completely forgot what my lover's hand would touch as it reached for moisture. I allowed him to descend, and then suddenly awoke to the realization that his fingers were in contact with my inflamed member. Utterly terrified, I wrenched my hips forward and tore his penis out of me. I jumped to my feet, pulling my panties up, expecting the blows to start falling. But when I looked at my Robin Hood, he was still on his knees, his tremendous tool outstretched before him. And instead of expressing fury, he was shaking with laughter.

"'You're not angry?' I asked.

"'Angry?' He could hardly speak for laughing.

"He controlled himself slightly. 'Why should I be angry of all things?'

"'Because I deceived you.'

"'But you haven't deceived me.'

"'I haven't—' I was dumbfounded. 'You mean you knew all along that I wasn't a woman?'

"'Of course I knew. Dear boy, as it has turned out, it's I who've deceived you.'

"'You? But how?'

"And, bursting into laughter once more, he rose to his feet, and from round his plump, fleshy hips unstrapped the belt to which was tied the pink rubber penis, perpetually erect. Once it was gone, what remained was a woman's triangle of hair adorning her loins.

"'You're a woman,' I said.

"'Of course I am. My name is Clara.'

"Now it was my turn to laugh, and I did so lengthily.

"'I came to this party,' she said, 'with the express aim of doing something I've always longed to do—to fuck a man. I hope you'll be good enough to allow me to complete a job that was so well begun.'

"'With the greatest pleasure.'

"She readjusted her dildo and we sank back into position. Once more the rubber penis was driven into my bowels, but this time, when Robin Hood's hand reached around, I waited with delight for Clara's fingers to circle my rod. Thus, pumping and pulling, Clara continued driving at me. She masturbated me while she fucked me in the ass; the combined pleasure was excruciating and exquisite. Every time she drove the dildo into my grasping butt, she jerked my tool. Within a few short moments the head of my cock had swollen to twice its normal size and my sperm was jetting onto the ground in thick gouts.

"Afterwards, she said, 'I realize that your tool is less mighty than mine, but I'm sure it can give me as much pleasure as mine has given you. If you don't mind, of course.'

"And, to show her how little I minded, I began at once to pull her costume from her. She joined the disrobing by pulling my gown from me. We were not still until Cinderella and Robin Hood lay flung upon the ground, and Clara and I stood facing each other. Her full, mature body glowed at me. My hands reached forward, circling her swollen globes. We drew closer, flesh meeting flesh, my cock firm against her belly. Our lips glued together, tongues circling. My fingers ran the length of her body, massaging each inch of her—the silky back, the resilient buttocks, the soft thighs.

"Without a word we dropped to the dew-laden grass, rolling over and over in the moisture, thighs hard against thighs. The cool dampness of the ground muddied and wet our flesh; soon Clara was everywhere as wet as she was between her legs. My hands rummaged in her, searched in her sweet pussy. I inserted my fingertip, drew it out, ran it again and again across her clitoris. Finally, her legs drew back. The pink lips gaped up at me. I bent over her, putting my penis at the threshold of her sheath. She trembled and I pushed, pushed, broke into her, joined our throbbing meat together, and thumped heavily, crazily. Her legs were in the air, spinning with her passion. I dove down into her, gasping at the feel of her tight pussy clutching at my shaft. My cock rammed the back of her womb and I pulled back and impaled her again. I steadied myself by grabbing her luscious breasts as I dropped my prick again and again into her dripping lovehole. Then, at the moment of our climax, her buttocks flailed up and down wildly so that nothing remained but the pouring of our juices.

"We remained locked together for some time.

"'I congratulate you,' she said at last.

"'Whatever for?'

"'For being as accomplished a husband as you are stimulating a wife.'

"'I can say no less for you. In fact, I really must say more—since you are easily twice as much of a husband as I am.'

"'Twice as much and half as much, since part of the time I am no husband at all.'

"'Nor am I.'

"'Yes,' she laughed. 'We are a strange couple. I

think we may look forward to many interesting evenings together. Isn't that so, my husband-wife?'

"'Indeed, my wife-husband.'

"When we returned to the ball, we danced a good deal and talked somewhat, telling each other of our past adventures. I, who until that evening had considered myself the most degenerate of creatures, was flabbergasted to learn of Clara's exploits. She had left nothing undone.

"'How remarkable you are,' I told her.

"'Why do you think so? Your life has been almost as full as mine. Besides, you are considerably younger than I.'

"'No, that's not what I mean. I say you're remarkable because debauchery has left no trace upon you. Your body is full and young, unblemished. Your face—well, I needn't describe your beauty. Certainly, dozens of others have made you aware of your charms.'

"'You flatter me.'

"'I don't. Why should I? But tell me, Clara, how do you manage to keep yourself so well, to show no trace of reckless living?'

"She sighed. 'Well, Rex, as I've told you, only a very restricted part of my life is devoted to my loves. When I return home each night, I go to bed and sleep until noon. My daughter, Angela, is at her studies then, and though we almost never see each other in the morning, I am very careful never to be absent from home.'

"'She has no idea of your—your second life?'

"'None whatsoever.'

"'How incredible that seems!'

"'Not at all. It has often cost a great deal to insure my secret. I've had to change servants regularly, and often pay heavily for their silence. Not that they have ever suspected anything. But it has unavoidably happened, of course, that a maid or a butler or Angela's governess has become aware of my absence during the night. It is easy to buy silence. They think I am a hysterically doting mother—'

"'Which, in fact, you seem to be.'

"'Yes, that's true. You see, my conduct isn't inconsistent. I tell the servants I have been to visit a friend, but that my daughter mustn't know. She must be certain that no one is more important to me than she is. And this is true.'

"'Yes, but how does this devotion keep you beautiful?'

"'It isn't devotion. It's simply that from the moment I rise at noon until I leave my home toward midnight, my life is peaceful, regular, ordered. I have eighteen hours of rest for every six hours of madness.'

"'I see.'

"'Most libertines, as you know, cannot keep their secrets for very long. They find it difficult to restrict their loves to a certain time. Their days are interrupted a dozen times and at any hour. This is what wears them out—not their actions, but that there is no regulation to their lives.'

"'I'll remember that,' I said.

"'If you do,' she told me, "and if you act accordingly, I think you'll find that your endurance is greater and that you'll be potent over a longer period of time than most men.'

"I realized then that Clara was someone who not only practiced sex, but also theorized about it. She had not, I could see, gone about her experience blindly as most do. When I asked her about this, she replied:

"'Would you expect me to ignore such a vital part of my life?'

"'I don't mean ignore...'

"'Most of the people at this party, no matter how debauched they are, and even though they think of nothing but sex, do actually ignore it.'

"'How do you mean?'

"'They think of it in terms of physical accomplishment. They dream up the wildest variations. Once I knew a man who taught me to make love standing on my head!'

"'Really? I've never heard of such a thing.'

"'Few people have. And yet there are cults all over the world who will do it no other way.'

"'You must teach it to me.'

"'I will, one day. But to get back to what I was saying, the man who taught me this saw in it only another exciting and violent way of fucking. For me, it was more than that—it was another achievement, a defiance of nature. A conquest.'

"'Of what?'

"'Of myself, if nothing else. Of my own limitations.'

"'I see.'

"'But for God's sake, Rex, please don't think I feel like a philosopher when I'm in the middle of lovemaking.'

"'You don't act like one.'

"'Thank you.'

"'And you certainly don't look like one.'

"'Now I'm really complimented.'

"The party ended, as those parties invariably do, in one tremendous orgy. Costumes were shredded and thrown into corners of the room. Mountains of throbbing flesh rose from floor to ceiling as people threw themselves upon each other. Clara, back to the role of Robin Hood, drove her rubber phallus into every opening that turned her way. I was always behind her, my relentless penis riding through the wet lips into her twitching sheath, my hands crushing the tense softness of her breasts.

"Somehow, in the course of the orgy, we were separated, for a man had come at her, torn her dildo away and dragged her off into another corner of the room. I heard her agonized shrieks over the noises of the crowd, heard the sound of her flesh being beaten. When I at last managed to crawl over to her, it was in time to see the man holding her hips in the air so that her body rested on her shoulders. He leaned forward between her thighs and plunged himself into her. His cock sank into her deeply. Then he took hold of her arms, pulled her into the air, and flung her back. The floor shook as she fell. Yet her legs held tight around the man's back so that nothing could break their contact.

"At that point I was interrupted in my watching, for two women and a man came rushing at me, dragging me to the ground.

"'It was not until much later that I saw Clara again. She came toward me, struggling with the man who had carried her away from me. His cock was still erect, inflamed. He wanted more.

"'Let me alone,' she kept shouting.

"'No.' He pulled her.

"'Find yourself someone else. I've got to leave now.'

"'You can't leave. The party will go on for days.'

"'I'll come back tomorrow then and we'll take up where we left off.'

"'I'll make you stay.'

"'You won't. Now don't be ridiculous. Let me alone. You can find yourself someone else.'

"'I'll let you alone,' he said to Clara, "if I can have HIM.'

"'Delighted,' I said.

"'You'll have to wait a minute,' said Clara. 'I must be going now, Rex,'

"'Can you come to my place tomorrow night?'

"'Yes.'

"I told her my address while she rummaged among some costumes. Since her own clothes were not to be found, she settled for a tiger skin which covered only one breast, leaving the other to stare at me enticingly.

"But then she was gone and Clara's former lover threw me to the ground, lifting me to the position he preferred. He spread my buttocks, drove his prick painfully into my bottom, and when we were secured together, he proceeded to fling me up and down as he had Clara. It didn't take long. I felt his penis grow, the blood in it throbbing against my flesh, and his cream burst into me. Since this satiated neither of us, we continued in exactly the same way well on into the morning.

"After this, we tired of each other and I decided to follow Clara's advice. I went home to sleep and rest, to prepare for my next encounter with the beautiful woman.

"She arrived at my room at midnight, bringing with her a man I had seen before, but could not place.

"Clara looked around my room and said, 'This is too small a room for good sex. Have you a bath?'

"'No, of course not.'

"She turned to the man. 'Buy Rex an apartment tomorrow. I'll pay you back in the evening.'

"He nodded.

"'We need room for love. And besides, we must have a bath. I'll teach you a marvelous way to make love. But first let me introduce you to my friend and business associate, Paul Lenoir.

"We shook hands, and I said, 'You know, I've seen you before, but I can't remember where.'

"'It's possible,' he replied. 'My job keeps me on the run.'

"'Paul,' Clara explained, 'is in the semen business.'

"'Really?' I couldn't help smiling.

"'I, too, was amused at first,' she said. 'But when you discover how his business will affect you, you will take it more seriously.'

"'It just seems a trifle odd,' I apologized.

"'In brief, what he does is buy and sell semen.'

"'Yes!' I exclaimed. 'That's how I happened to see him.'

"'Really?' Lenoir asked me. 'I don't remember having done business with you.'

"'No, you haven't. But several months ago, I was walking down the street with a friend, and you passed on the opposite side. My friend pointed you out to me and said, 'Do you see that fellow? He's a most extraordinary creature. He was sent to me a few weeks ago by a friend. He offered me 2,000 francs for a bottle of joy-juice. Not a big bottle at that—two or three days' work at most. I said I'd be delighted to oblige, but that it was quite a bit to ask a girl if she wouldn't mind giving back what I'd just bestowed upon her. He gave me a box of rubbers and told me to use them then empty them into the bottle, or simply give him the used rubbers. Needless to say, I agreed and I've been filling bottles galore ever since.' My friend didn't tell me what you do with the stuff.'

"'I resell it,' said Lenoir.

"'And I'm one of his most regular clients,' Clara informed me.

"'And what do you do with it?' I asked her.

"'That, you will learn tomorrow.'

"'As a matter of fact,' said Lenoir, 'Clara is my

most demanding client. I've had to give up a number of others to keep her orders filled.'

"'That isn't true, Paul. Once I had the amount I needed, it was only a question of a small, steady supply.'

"'I certainly am anxious to know,' I said, 'to what uses you put the stuff.'

"'You'll have to wait. Now, before we get down to tonight's business, I want you to remember to have all your things packed by midnight tomorrow. I'll come round with a taxi and take you to your new quarters.' She turned to Lenoir. 'You'll be sure to find something really excellent for him?'

"'Have I ever failed you, Clara?'

"'No, you haven't—not in any way.'

"And so, the three of us undressed and had a party that lasted until dawn. Clara was magnificent and Lenoir and I took full advantage of her charms. I situated myself between her legs while Lenoir took up a position by her head. Then, when I plunged my cock into her pouting quim, he drove his cock deep into her throat and we began to double-fuck her. Clara exulted in this. She grabbed Lenoir's long, thin tool and pumped it while she licked around the head and shaft. She moved down to the balls and massaged his sac with her tongue before returning to the tip again. Then she throated him and sucked him with the practiced muscles there, drawing a groan from him as he felt his very essence drawn from his balls. All this time I was working between her thighs, plunging my rock-hard cock in and out of her pussy. I still couldn't believe my good fortune. Not only was I getting to fuck a beautiful woman who loved to have cocks driven into her every orifice, I was going to be given an apartment too. My excitement mounted and I rammed my pole harder, delighting in the way Clara's tits bounced with each thrust.

"We continued this way, switching positions of course, until Clara indicated she had to prepare for the activities of the day to come. Lenoir and I each finished, spilling another load of sperm into Clara's pussy, mouth, or anus, and made the final preparations for my move.

"Needless to say, I was thrilled at the idea of leaving my little room for a spacious apartment. All my packing was done hours before Clara was due to arrive. I spent the evening pacing back and forth across the floor waiting for the great moment.

"At last she came, Lenoir and the cabbie behind her.

"'Are you ready?' she asked.

"'Ready? I've been packed since the afternoon.'

"'Good. Shall we go along then?'

"We each took a valise, left the room and went down the stairs into the street. We climbed into the taxi and were on our way in a moment.

"'I'm thrilled about all this,' I said, hardly able to believe it was actually happening.

"'Wait until you've seen the place!' said Clara.

"'Have *you* seen it?' I asked.

"'We've just come from there. And it's all yours.'

"'God, Clara,' I said, 'I can't think of any way to thank you!'

"'Don't be silly. It's a pleasure for me. And besides, you simply had to have a place with a bath.'

"When the cab came to a stop, I was astonished to see we were just across the street from the Tuileries.

"'Surely it isn't here?' I said.

"'Of course it is. And what's more, it has a view upon the gardens.'

"We all went upstairs and Clara gave me the key.

"'I think you ought to carry me across the threshold,' she said.

"I opened the door, picked her up in my arms and carried her into the flat.

"'Furnished,' I cried. I was incredulous to see that nothing was wanting in the apartment.

"'Of course, furnished. I thought it would be such a bore to have to waste time buying furniture.'

"We went round the apartment, Lenoir and the driver still with us. I had noticed that Clara seemed interested in the driver. He was a good-looking man—but more than that, he was a potential sexual partner, and that was enough to interest Clara. As we made our way around the flat, I saw her edge close to him and whenever possible wiggle her buttocks against him. The poor man seemed half-mad with desire. When we reached the bathroom, Clara suddenly turned to the man and said:

"'We're going to have a little party here tonight.' Her leg moved against his. 'A very *intimate* party, you understand. Perhaps you'd like to stay?'

"'I'd love to,' he said in a hoarse whisper.

"And so Clara told him everyone's name, and he in turn said he was called Louis.

"'Well, then, gentlemen,' Clara began, turning the knob of the bathroom door, 'allow me to present the treat of the evening.'

"She threw open the door. It was the most spectacular bathroom I had ever seen: larger than an ordinary sitting-room. And it was furnished not only with a tub, but with a large bed and a couch.

"'Come closer,' she said. 'Come closer. And see what's in the tub.'

"Louis and I approached. The tub was half-filled with a thick, gleaming, milky fluid. It took me several seconds to realize what it was.

"'So *that's* why you were so anxious for a bath,' I said.

"'Exactly.'

"'But it must be terribly cold.'

"'Not at all,' she replied, and turned to Lenoir. 'Paul, will you warm the bath?'

"'Certainly.' He left the room.

"While he was gone, Clara reached her hand into the tub, stroked the thick fluid, then took her dripping fingers out, patting them across my face and that of Louis, the driver.

"'What is it?' he asked, taken aback.

"'What does it look like?'

"'I-I'm not sure.'

"Drawing herself close to him, she said, 'It's what you'll soon be pouring into me.'

"Louis' arms went around Clara and their mouths sucked together in a passionate kiss. I watched his hands fondle her back from thigh to shoulder.

"When Lenoir returned he was carrying with him a curious device—two long metal rods fastened together and from whose top appeared a long wire which ultimately tapered into a plug. This plug he shoved into a socket not far from the tub, and then he plunged the twin rods into the bath of semen.

"'As the rods heat up,' Clara explained, 'the liquid is warmed. God bless the machine age. Let's undress.'

"So the four of us began to disrobe one another. When we were naked, Clara once again reached into the tub.

"'It's almost ready,' she said. 'Who will smear my body with the precious stuff?'

"She had three volunteers, so it was decided that since Louis was the newcomer, he would coat Clara. But since actually it was my great evening, Clara, once coated, would cover me with the liquid.

"Louis was enraptured. He approached Clara, his hands and thick tool outstretched. Again, their bodies met, and as they kissed he wriggled until his penis moved in between her thighs. They shimmied and rubbed and stroked and sighed. At last, Clara broke away. 'No, no, you terrible man. I must first of all be covered with the most precious—and expensive—juice in the world.'

"Moving to the tub, Louis reached his hands into the fluid, then drew them out and began massaging Clara. He put the stuff upon her shoulders and rubbed downwards across her chest. He coated her breasts thickly so that they were like milky blobs. Taking more fluid, he stroked her belly and hips, and with two great handfuls smeared the hair of her loins into a gluey mess. Clara was now dripping with come. Louis' ecstatic wet hand reached between her thighs, and Clara leaned against the wall, raising herself so that we could all see the area upon which he worked. Her cunt was thick with sperm and Louis' fingers moved into her slit. Then he painted her thighs, her knees, ankles, even between her toes.

"She turned around saying, 'Now the second part.'

"Louis willingly obeyed. Soon her back dripped with the juice of a thousand orgasms. Delicately, Louis spread her buttocks and massaged the cream there and into her anus. Soon she was one mass of already-drying semen.

"'Now, Rex...'

"'Yes.'

"'It's your turn to feel the delicious moisture on every part of your body.'

"Her hands swooped into the bath, cupping out masses of the liquid. She was less economical and in a much greater hurry than Louis had been. The warm, sticky mess came pasting upon my body in thick patches; it ran down my neck, chest and legs. With two handfuls she fondled my genitals. The sensation was so pleasant I thought I might at any moment add to Clara's supply. But, in fact, she was done with me almost before she began.

"'That was much too quick,' I said.

"'But I wanted to finish before it dried.'

"Her face came close to me, and with passion burning in her eyes she began licking from my body what she had just applied to it. She drank from my chest and armpits, from my navel, from my thickly-coated loins, from my legs, from my back, from between my buttocks. Her tongue flickered out hungrily, her lips sucked along each inch of my fevered body.

"When I was licked clean, Clara removed the electric rods from the tub and said, 'Come, Rex. Come into the bath.' She stepped in and I followed her, sinking my body into the thick jelly of joy.

"'Isn't it marvelous?' Clara shrieked, splashing both herself and me with the fluid.

"Paul Lenoir and Louis knelt beside us and rubbed us with our bathwater. I stretched my hands forward, through the thick mess, and sought Clara's slippery breasts. I squeezed them, tugging her large nipples. She in turn took hold of my penis, pulling at it in the velvety softness of the semen. Now and then a rubber contraceptive floated to the surface, and Clara grabbed it and slid it across her face.

"'Think of all the love we're lying in,' she cried with mad delight.

"When one of the rubbers surfaced, she took hold of it, and told Louis to stand up. When he obeyed, she opened the rubber and drew it on to his member, rubbing her sperm-laden hands across his scrotum. Then Louis pushed his organ toward

Clara's face; her mouth opened and the dripping rubber-covered penis burst into her mouth. She sucked at it hungrily.

"While she did this, I moved forward, lying down between her legs. I threw her knees back and felt her jellied twat under the liquid. I moved on top of her, edged my rod to her burning pussy and lunged forward, carrying with me a dozen orgasms. Just as we joined together, Lenoir leaped into the tub, jumped on top of me and plunged his heated mass into my twitching asshole. To complete the party, Louis came into the bath, never removing his rubber-coated prick from Clara's devoted mouth. The four of us jumped and shook and twitched. Lenoir pounded in and out of me, and I pounded in and out of Clara while I clutched her tits and rolled her nipples between my fingers. At last we all came to our climax, and our fresh juices mixed with the juices in the tub.

"Clara stretched languidly. 'Isn't life wonderful?' she said.

"Yes, life was wonderful, but the tub had begun to grow chilly, so we all jumped out and thrust the electric rods back in to heat the stuff.

"We bundled up close together in a kind of weird dance, shivering across each other's jellied body. Clara was delighted to lick us all clean, and when she tore the rubber off Louis' penis she pushed the head into her mouth and sucked it until it emerged spotless. This so enflamed Louis that he dropped himself to the floor between Clara's legs and drank passionately at her cunt. After a moment she moved away, arranging herself above Louis' member. Gracefully, she descended upon it, fixing its length in herself. As they sat thus, Lenoir and I began scooping up semen and showering it upon the lovers. (In fact, Lenoir threw such an excessive amount that I could not help suspecting he had one eye on his business.)

"As Clara leaned forward over Louis, her breasts swayed and I filled the valley between them with joy-juice. Then I filled my own behind with come and planted my bottom squarely on Louis's face, bending forward so that my own mouth covered Clara's moist tit. To my delight, I felt Louis' tongue licking at the substance I'd placed at his disposal. Lenoir joined us by plunging his anointed instrument into Clara's mouth. We all bounced savagely, and to insure my orgasm, I removed my behind from Louis' mouth and substituted my cock. I was surprised at the expertise he showed sucking my prick. He was as experienced as any woman I'd known. I, however, wasn't going to ask any questions. I simply luxuriated in the wonderful feeling of having my cock sucked by the mouth of another person, man or woman I didn't care. I began to fuck his mouth the way I would Clara's cunt, had I been in that position. I thrust in and out, enjoying the way he lapped at the semen dripping from my shaft and cockhead. He flicked at the slit in the tip of my knob and throated me in three deep strokes that had me adding my own deposit to that milky accumulation. He gulped it all eagerly. The four of us once again poured away our juices.

"Afterwards, the bath had warmed and we climbed back into the restful jelly, playing with gentle exhaustion.

"'Wouldn't it be marvelous,' said Clara, 'if we could identify every drop of this semen?'

"'What do you mean?' I asked.

"'Well, suppose I pointed to that drop on your nose and told you it was from the time that Joseph fucked Lucy in her father's garage. It would be so nice to know each instance of every drop.'

"'Your curiosity is insatiable,' said Lenoir. 'How much can you expect me to ask of my laborers?'

"Clara laughed. 'Oh, I don't expect you to ask! I just think it would be marvelous to know. Here hundreds of people have come thousands of times and we sit in it all and don't know under what circumstances it was made.'

"'Well,' Louis told her, 'you can be sure that from now on I'll save every trickle for you and tell you exactly how it happened.'

"'I'd like that,' Clara said, rubbing his back with the sticky fluid.

"'I know where you can collect a lot of it—and get it for nothing,' Louis said to Clara.

"Lenoir was obviously displeased. 'I'm sure that I've left no stone unturned in my quest for the vital liquid.'

"'I'll bet this is a place you never went to,' Louis challenged. 'Because few people even know about it.'

"'Where is it?' Clara asked.

"'It's an old soldier's organization. They have a monthly meeting, and after the meeting there's a party in the back. A couple of men and women come out and fuck in the middle of the room and the old guys sit around watching and whacking off.'

"'Are there a lot of them?' Clara asked.

"'About a hundred. And they go at it three or four times during the performance.'

"'How can we collect it?' said Clara.

"'Leave that to me. If you're willing to give a performance, I'll take care of the rest.'

"'I'd be delighted,' she said.

"'There's going to be a meeting a week from today. The show starts about one o'clock, so I'll pick you up here at, say, half-past twelve.'

"'That's fine.'

"Having settled the business, we returned to pleasure, and continued with it until it was time for Clara to leave. When they'd all gone, I settled down to the problem of unpacking.

"Clara visited me every night during the week that followed and she invariably brought two or three people with her. She was, I must confess, the least discriminating of individuals. As far as love was concerned, Clara was truly blind. She would bring fat prostitutes and old vagabonds, in fact anyone she chanced upon. And curiously enough, each person flowered under her touch. Thrust into a steaming bath of semen, a pimply boy could become the most violent of lovers.

"Thus, the week of waiting passed. As he had promised, Louis appeared at my door at half-past midnight.

"'We've got to hurry,' he said.

"'We're ready,' Clara told him, and she and I followed him down to his cab. Clara sat with him in the front seat and sucked him all the way to the meeting place. It was funny the way the car jerked and swerved as Clara licked and throated Louis' upstanding tool.

"We parked in an alley behind a large building, climbed a very dark staircase, then entered a nondescript room which ultimately led into a tremendous hall where scores of chairs were arranged in a large circle around a small space.

"'They'll be here in a minute,'' said Louis. It was only then I noticed he had a large box in his hand.

"'What's that?' I asked him.

"'It's to collect the sperm. Wait, I think I hear them.'

"A large door in the back of the room burst open and the veterans entered in a rush. They were all

176

sizes, shapes and ages, and I could hear their heavy, anxious breathing. In a group they walked to a corner of the room and there proceeded to remove their clothing, each putting his things into a little locker-like box which had apparently been constructed for these occasions.

"When they were nude they came forward and took their seats. Louis raised his arms, bringing the men to silence.

"'Tonight, gentlemen,' Louis began, 'I've brought for your pleasure someone who is not only the most beautiful woman many of us have had the pleasure to gaze upon, but is also the most spectacular.'

"The audience leaned forward.

"'I take pride,' continued Louis, 'in presenting Clara, the insatiable.'

"The men applauded appreciatively as Louis said to us it was time to undress. This was done at length and with infinite slowness. Of course, Clara attracted a great deal more attention that we did. The men couldn't tear their eyes from her magnificent breasts, her long legs, and the delicious mossing of hair on her mount. When the three of us were completely naked, Louis once more began to speak.

"'Now, tonight, gentlemen, you are in for a very special treat. Clara is a passionate collector of that juice which is such a delight for men to produce. In this box which I've brought along with me are hundreds of rubbers. Clara herself will place them on your throbbing cocks. I have enough caps to go around six times. Now, this is the special treat of the evening: to any or all of you men capable of two orgasms, Clara will let you deposit a third, a fourth, and even a fifth and sixth—into the beautiful slit which I shall now reveal to you.'

"Louis lifted Clara up in the air, her back to his

chest. I, in turn, stepped forward, stooping, and spread Clara's thighs wide to the audience. Her pussylips were open for inspection and smiled pinkly at the men. We circled the room while the men sighed with appreciation.

"'Now, gentlemen,' said Louis, 'if you will permit, she will cover your thundering erections with the rubbers.'

"Louis tore the box open and we passed around the room. while Clara stopped before each of the hundred men, moistened their cockheads with her mouth, and rolled the rubbers over them. No man could resist fingering the flesh that had so recently been displayed to him.

"When all the rods in the room, save mine and Louis', had been covered, we three performers returned to the center of the floor and began the rites of love. Clara was superb that evening. Every inch of her body trembled with excitement. Passion radiated from her, and I myself became so crazed with desire that I felt I could easily add a half-dozen orgasms to her collection. Louis and I labored over her and the three of us rolled on the floor, coming close to the men whose hands reached out. My mouth sealed upon one of Clara's tits; Louis' mouth sealed upon the other. My hand rode down her body, exploring it anew, finding her flesh for the first time under two hundred watching eyes. My fingers dug downward, clawing into her wet, pink womanhood; and another hundred hands reached with mine.

"The three of us turned on our side. I was in front of Clara and Louis was in back. Simultaneously, we began the penetration of her body. Her left leg was raised high in the air so that all those watching could observe the head of my aching cock slide into the widening sheath. Just behind this, another penis was entering into her. We lunged, driving ourselves in to the hilt. The room was alive with passionate sighs. Again and again I plunged myself in and out of her, and Louis followed suit. Her leg remained fixed in space so that our contact was freely revealed. All the men stood up and moved forward, closing the circle around us so that the hot breath of their excitement poured down. Their eyes remained fixed on the way her dripping pussylips expanded and contracted on my ravaging prick. All the while Louis drilled her willing bumhole. In this heated, fevered mass, we flung ourselves at Clara. I continued pounding in and out of her cunt. My excitement grew to the bursting point at the realization that I was fucking this gorgeous creature in full sight of a hundred horny men who would trade anything they owned to be in my place. I wriggled my prick around so as to stretch her quim more and open it to their sight. The slit grinned pinkly and made a moist sucking sound as my cock slid back and forth like a bow on a violin. Louis, meanwhile, wasn't quite as conscientious in his ministrations. He simply banged the hell out of Clara's asshole, ramming his prick in and out again and again until I could feel the force of his thrusts all the way on the other side of Clara's gleaming nude body. We began to spurt into her, our spasms visible to the lusting men. In a moment there was nothing but the sighs of more than a hundred orgasms in a hundred rubbers.

"The men returned to their seats and Clara stood up and went around the room collecting the used rubbers, knotting them and depositing them in a corner. In this way, each man had the supreme delight of being licked clean by Clara's ever-hungry tongue. Afterwards, she returned to place fresh rubbers on all of them.

"A second performance ensued, with variations on the first. This time, Clara held Louis' prick and my own in each of her hands, and by turning her head from side to side, sucked us off alternately. First she turned to the left and popped his engorged cockhead into her mouth. But only for a moment. Then she swung to the right and slid my pole into her mouth. And so it went, back and forth until both our tools were jumping and straining to release the load of sperm that boiled in our balls. She concluded the performance by jamming both of our cocks into her mouth at the same time while we ejaculated. She pumped us until we'd been milked dry and swallowed every drop without difficulty. Ultimately another hundred caps were filled.

"'And now, gentlemen,' Louis said, "the rest of the evening is yours. Each of you may use Clara as you see fit.'

"It was now time for Louis and me to retire to the audience's position. What ensued was a free-for-all such as I have never, before or since, seen. The more assailed Clara was, the more responsive she became. The more orgasms she was driven to, the more she desired. Penises covered and filled every part of her flesh. She was bitten and flailed, scratched and torn, and she merely screamed for more. She had an enormous cock up her cunt, one jammed in her asshole, another in her mouth, one between her breasts, and one in each of her hands. I've never seen any one woman fucked by so many raging cocks. Clara was barely visible under all that meat. And when the orgasms erupted, the room was a battleground of rocketing sperm and cries of passion. More men took the places of the first group and the orgy resumed at the same frantic pace. Clara literally oozed come from every orifice.

"But Louis and I, I must confess, were not long watching. There were a couple of dozen men who thought it an excellent idea to keep their irons, as it were, in our fires—until Clara's furnace was ready to receive them. Needless to say, I found this highly enjoyable. I never sucked so many cocks, rammed my tool up so many asses, and was in turn reamed by so many.

"In all, it was an extravagant evening. Clara left at dawn, and Louis and I soon followed with several hundred rubber-wrapped orgasms. He drove me home in his taxi and helped bring the semen up to the flat where, as exhausted as we were, we managed to coax each other into increasing Clara's supply ever-so-slightly.

"But, strangely enough, Clara never returned to my flat. Nor did Louis. The only time I ever saw her again was a month later when it occurred to me she might return to the scene of her greatest orgy. Truly, she was there with Louis and several other men; the soldiers had not yet come in.

"'Clara,' I called.

"'Oh, Rex, my darling.'

"'What's happened?'

"'Nothing's happened!'

"She seemed so casual I couldn't think what to say to her.

"'Why should you think anything's happened?' she asked.

"'It's been a month since I've seen you.'

"'I know.'

"'Well, why haven't you come to the flat?'

"'Frankly, Rex, ever since that first night here. I've realized that one, two, three, or even ten men just aren't enough for me. I need a mob—like this.'

"'But this is only once a month.'

"'*This* is. But Louis knows of parties like this all over Paris—night after night.'

"'I see.'

"I stayed around for the party that night and promised Clara I would come to the others whose addresses she gave me. But I never did go. The truth is, I'd grown fond of her and wanted her for myself—at least now and then. Since this was impossible, I thought it wiser to break the attachment immediately.

"The next day I had a woman sent in to clean my bathtub. It had become a cruddy mess during its unused month and the woman grumbled and complained that she had never seen a bath in such a frightful state. She didn't seem to know what the rubbers were.

"What are all these things?' she asked. 'Dried-up balloons?'

"'Are you married?'

"'Yes. And with ten kids.'

"'Ah, that explains it.'

"She shrugged and finished cleaning. When she left I gave her the twin electric rods as a present, telling her they heated water in no time.

"And so, Mr. Cunningham, Clara's last trace disappeared from my apartment—and my life."

"She came a long way from the time I knew her," I told Baxter.

"But you weren't shocked by my story."

"Good heavens, no."

"Then I can only say that what you've heard from others about Clara must have prepared you for this."

"Yes, indeed. Well, Mr. Baxter, I won't trouble you any more."

"It's been no trouble at all. In fact I've enjoyed every minute of it."

We stood up and he showed me out of the salon.

"Just one more thing," I said.

"Anything."

"Might I see your bath?"

Baxter burst into laughter. "But of course," he said, and led me into the room.

CHAPTER
SEVEN

VII.

There remained but two visits to make, and I must confess I felt disinclined to make them. As Clara's life—or the stories of it—delved more and more deeply into the patterns of degeneracy, I felt less and less involved with her, with the memory of her. I had found Baxter's tale faintly unpleasant; but I had not been moved. Clara's revenge had overstepped itself.

Still, I was determined to do the "honorable" thing. I would go on with the visits.

The fifth name on the list belonged to a woman named Emma Deligny. Her address and telephone number indicated that she lived in the Montmartre area. I waited two days before I telephoned her, and it took considerable effort of will to force myself to dial her number.

"Hello!" a woman's voice screamed at me.

"Hello, may I speak with Emma Deligny?"

"Emma, Emma, Emma," she muttered. "I *am* Emma." She sounded uncertain of this.

"You are Emma Deligny?"

"No."

What an exasperating person. "Are you Emma Deligny?"

"Sometimes." She sighed deeply, and for an instant I thought she was going to burst into tears. "My name is Howard Cunningham," I said, hoping this might mean something to her.

"I'm not well," she said softly.

"I'm sorry to hear that. I'm calling you to ask if you might remember a woman named Clara."

"Emma."

"No, not Emma—Clara. You are Emma."

"Yes."

"Do you think I might come by this afternoon to speak to you for a few moments?"

There was only silence at the other end of the line so I repeated my question.

"What did you say?" she asked.

"I would like to talk to you about Clara."

There was more silence. When I was once again about to speak, I heard her scream.

"What's the matter?" I shouted.

"Where is she? Where is she?"

"Where is who?"

"Where is Clara? When is she coming home? Emma is waiting."

"I'll be right over," I said to her.

"With Clara?"

I hung up without answering, went out, climbed into my car and drove to Montmartre. The house was on a curious street, like a farm road right in the middle of the city. I went through the gate and up to the house; it was a private residence and it was more than half in ruins.

Having knocked at the door, I waited, ill at ease. It

was not long before I once again heard the voice that had assailed me over the telephone.

"Clara?" it asked.

Ridiculously, I replied, "Yes."

The door opened a crack and a face peered out at me. It was so white and the room behind it so dark that I had a momentary impression of a disembodied head. The face was old, old, the oldest face I could remember having seen. It was ghastly white, hung in great fleshy folds, the eyes and mouth slanted downward. The hair that bordered the face was a painful, alarmingly bright violet. It was tinted to match her huge crazed eyes.

"Clara?" she asked looking at me.

I could think of nothing to say. A finger appeared below the face; she crooked it at me, inviting me to enter. I obeyed and she shut the door behind me. I could see absolutely nothing in the darkness. I waited, then heard flat, unpleasant footsteps flop across the room. A door opened and a flood of light burst out at me. In the light I saw the woman who let me in.

She was naked but for a wide band around her flabby upper arm. What I noticed first was the hair at her loins had been dyed the same color as the hair on her head. I had a momentary impression of this madwoman sitting on a bidet full of purple ink, dipping her fleshy parts into the color. Her body was revolting. Long, thin breasts hung to her belly and ended in enormous nipples that had been painted red; her navel was the same color. Fold after fold of pleated flesh hung from her—and yet she wasn't fat. Once, no doubt, she *had* been, but the substance was gone and there remained now only this hideous wrinkled coat of skin.

I followed her into the room whose door she had

opened. A score of bulbs burned nakedly and scorched my eyes. When I could control my vision I looked around the room. Every inch of wall and window had been pasted over with photographs of Clara, lurid photographs which made Van Drooft's seem like professional portraits. An unmade bed occupied most of the room, but there was also a stool and a dressing table upon which stood the telephone. The mirror over the table had been pasted up with photographs of Clara.

"Where is Clara?" she asked me suddenly.

"When was the last time you saw her?"

She sank to the edge of the bed and her thighs moved apart, revealing her slit.

"The last time?" she asked herself. "Last night. We had a party last night. They all came."

"It couldn't have been last night," I said softly.

Her face was full of hatred. "I tell you it was last night," she screamed. "You were here too. I remember. You were the one we nailed to the wall." She jumped up suddenly. "Have you got it?"

"Got what?"

She started digging at my trousers and I backed away in horror.

"You *have* got it," she cried. "I felt it. When Clara comes back we'll finish you off. We'll take it away from you."

I realized there would be little use in trying to talk to this woman, but I made one desperate effort to penetrate her mind.

"Clara said," I told her, "that you were to tell me about that party."

"Don't lie to me," she sneered. "You managed to get away. You managed to live. You still have your bomb. Let me see it."

"No."

189

"Fuck me and then I'll cut it off."

Then she tried to tempt me. She moved around the room, mincing and waltzing. She dropped herself upon the bed, let her hands stray across the flat breasts, circle over the belly and draw wide the lips of her ravaged womanhood.

"Put it into me here," she moaned and began to cry.

I was repelled. "No, I'm afraid I'll have to be leaving."

"Fuck me a little; just a very little," she sighed through her tears.

I confess that I was saddened by her. I said, "If I do, will you tell me about the party?"

"Yes, all about the party. There were so many of them. There were so many people."

I approached her and stood at the side of the bed. Her hands came away from her loins, reached to my trousers and undid the buttons. When she pulled my underwear down, I closed my eyes and let her play with my cock. It seemed like hours before it began to stiffen and rise. Her damp hands stroked me tenderly. With my eyes still closed, I lifted myself over her. The soft hand led my member to the flaming sheath.

"All at once," she hissed. "It must go in all at once."

She raised her body, set my penis, and then thrust herself forward so that when contact was made I was forced in to the hilt.

My scream echoed against the walls.

I have never known such agony as I experienced at that moment. It was as if blades were cutting into my penis. Opening my eyes, I stared down at the woman's insane face. I was afraid to move, fearing that I might damage myself seriously, but the pain was so intense I couldn't think of leaving it in. With one blast of courage I pulled myself back, going through hell as my organ emerged. When it was completely withdrawn I looked down at it. I thought I would faint at the sight of it. It was a mess of scratches and abrasions; blood came from some of the cuts.

Emma Deligny's eyes were wide open and she stared with incredible excitement at my bruised member.

"More," she sighed. "More."

I wouldn't even answer her, and suddenly I saw her body begin to shake and tremble. Her knees shot open and closed, bringing her flabby thighs together again and again. I could tell, of course, that she was approaching her climax, and yet her eyes never moved from my instrument, which I was now wiping clean with my handkerchief.

"Oh, oh," she sobbed. "Look how you suffer."

Her body heaved itself into the air and the bed groaned under her fall. Again she heaved. Her thighs sprang together more and more rapidly and her moans were more frequent and noisier. At that moment I noticed the glass pitcher on her dressing table. Approaching it, I saw that it was full of coffee, turned cold. I took the pitcher up, returned to the woman, and as she throbbed toward her orgasm I poured the coffee in one big splash on her body.

She sat up enraged, trying to catch her breath.

"What hideous device," I shouted, "have you got in your cunt, you filthy woman?"

This seemed to calm her down, and she said, "It hurt you. It tore you."

"Not as badly, perhaps, as you would have liked."

I adjusted my trousers and started to the door of the room. She jumped out of the bed and moved between me and the door.

"Clara," she said remembering. "Did you bring Clara?"

"Yes," I told her. "She's outside. I'll tell her to come in."

With one violent wrench, I pulled her from the door, went from the room and through the dark hall, and fled from the house, slamming the door behind me.

Away...let me get away. Let me get away.

The words turned over and over in my head as my car sped from the street to the boulevard.

CHAPTER EIGHT

VIII.

It was not from potential disgust but from sheer terror that I decided not to pay my sixth visit. The minutes I spent with Emma Deligny left me with a vivid impression of cumulative horror, of Clara's life going in a determined line toward greater and greater perversion—ending in death by perversion.

I felt that the sixth name on Clara's list might involve personal danger to myself, so it was with a sense of terror and uncertainty that I told myself I would not make the final call. Still, the problem turned itself over and over in my mind, and by the time I thought my decision definite, I was once more thrust into doubt by finding the newspaper that had first told me of Clara's death.

That night I dreamed about her, but this dream was altogether different from the other, the one that had come to me at the first stages of my quest. In this one, Clara wept. Nothing existed but her weeping.

I asked her why she was crying. But she wouldn't reply. Instinctively I realized the nature of her problem. She was dead. That one particular aspect of her life—its end—remained for me a mystery.

When I woke, I knew there was no alternative. And so, that very day I rode upon a plane, a train, and a bus, and at four in the afternoon I arrived at the marketplace of Naire, a small village not an hour away from the Spanish border. I left my bag in the hamlet's only hotel and asked the proprietor where I might find the Villa des Fleurs.

"Are you going up there?" he asked.

"Yes."

"It will be no use. He sees no one."

"Who are you talking about?"

"Well, the master of the villa—Monsieur Montrose."

That was the name on Clara's list: Serge Montrose.

"Yes," I said to the proprietor. "That's who I'm going to see."

"He won't see you. The servants will never let you through the gate."

"Nevertheless, I'll try."

He shrugged and indicated the small road that led out of the village. There was no way to Montrose's place except by foot. Since it was a good climb, I started out at once. It was a beautiful walk and I could see the villa a half-hour before I reached it. Placed like a citadel on a sloping hill, its view governed the village.

The house was well-named, for flowers lay everywhere around it. When I approached the gate, I admired the well-kept lawn, then pulled at the bell. A servant-girl opened the front door, came down to see me, but kept the gate locked between us.

"Yes?" she asked.

"I've come to see Monsieur Montrose."

"I'm sorry, but Monsieur Montrose sees no one."

"He may be willing to see me. Will you tell him that Howard Cunningham, an American friend of Clara's, would like to have a few words with him?"

"I'm sorry but—"

"Please ask him!"

She turned and went back into the house, leaving the door open behind her. I was kept waiting a considerable time before I saw anyone come back into the doorway. This time it was not the girl, but an enormous old man. His bulk hung on the threshold. His fat face bore a huge white beard and where he wasn't bald his hair was white and long.

"What do you want?" he roared at me across the distance.

"Are you Montrose?"

"Why do you want to know?"

"I come at the request of Clara."

"She's dead."

I nodded, but decided to be silent and wait for his move. His accent surprised me, for although he bore a French name he didn't have a French accent. Also there was something about his presence that stirred my memory.

"I won't see you," he shouted. "Go back where you came from."

On a wild hunch, I yelled back at him, "If I leave without seeing you, you'll have reason to regret it, Baron Arvon."

He came straight down the path and opened the gate for me. "She told you?" he hissed at me.

"Yes," I lied.

We looked at each other with equal amounts of disgust.

"If she weren't already dead," he said, "I would kill her again."

"Again?" The word shook me.

"How much do you want?" he said coldly.

"I don't want anything from you."

"What have you come here for?"

"To find Clara's murderer."

"Murderer," he said with a sneer. "There was no murder involved. It was a pleasure for us both."

"Especially for you, I suppose."

He had moved away from the gate and dropped his huge body into a chair on the lawn. I sat down beside him.

"She told you about our arrangement?" he asked me.

"No."

"Then how did you know—"

I thought more quickly than I ever had. "She left me a letter before her death." This was as ambiguous as I could make it.

"I'll tell you then, Mr. Cunningham, that twenty years ago I was going to kill her. She begged me not to because of our child, but since I could no longer bear living with her, and since I couldn't face the disgrace of a public separation, it was decided that I would 'die' instead. In exchange for this I would have the honor of killing her in my own fashion on her fortieth birthday. So my death took place. I bought new papers, a new identity, and this villa where I spend only part of my time. I make frequent visits to other places—in fact, during the past twenty years I've made frequent visits to Clara. She even told me of her love for you. *Love for you!* No one in all these past twenty years had ever done for Clara what I could do, what I *did* do, from the night we were married to the night she died."

"I want you to tell me about her death."

"And then you'll tell the police?"

"No. You'll tell them."

"I'll make a deal with you, Cunningham. I'll tell you about Clara's death, but in exchange for it you'll let me destroy myself. You won't tell the police."

"I can't agree. You seem to be an expert at living after death."

"You can take my word. Accept my deal, not for my sake, but for the sake of my name—and for the daughter."

I felt no sympathy at all for him, but I thought that it would, should I not accept his offer, only mean useless pain for Angela.

"All right. I agree," I told him.

"Good. I'm grateful."

"Never mind your gratitude. Tell me about the murder."

"It was simple. The arrangement had been that on her fortieth birthday, Clara would take a room at a certain hotel whose owner was well-paid for his silence. Soon after she entered the room, I followed her with the curious alcohol that the police discovered. I also brought with me the enormous penis in which Clara rejoiced and an iron rod. I lit the alcohol burner and placed the rod on top of the heat.

"We undressed. Clara had grown lovelier with every year. Maturity had brought to her body what little it might have lacked in youth. Who has seen anything so superb as those ever-swelling breasts that bloomed out, round, firm, yielding? I stroked her nipples, feeling them stiffen in my fingers. Throwing her to her knees, I forced my cock into her mouth; it was an easy task for her to take all of it—an easy and delightful one. Her plump lips pressed upon it; her moist tongue licked it; the flesh of her mouth yielded its heat to my stiffness. Then she licked at my balls, her tongue flickering at my sac.

"She lay down upon the floor and I joined her, pushing my face into that oily groove I knew so well. I rubbed it with my head, then put my tongue to it, sliding along the length of the slit, tickling her clitoris, plunging into the wide, expectant gap.

"'Your moment has come,' I said.

"'Hurry, I can't wait.'

"Even the prospect of death was not enough to lessen her excitement.

"Her knees drew back and I moved between her thighs. My prick was at her door. I tapped gently, entered slightly, drew back, entered again, withdrew again. Her hole twitched for my full penetration, and at last I lowered myself, easing my member into the depths of her body. Her mouth dribbled with her passion. She clutched at me and we drove at each other fiercely, my tool pounding her. I fucked her as never before, granting her that last singular moment of pleasure that I'd promised her. She met my every thrust with one of her own, equally strong, equally desirous of that inevitable end that she knew approached. She wanted it, I tell you, though I am sure you will not believe me. Even as my cock filled her magnificent pussy she yearned for her death and the new sensation that would accompany it. You think me cruel, insane perhaps, but I am not. I simply gave her what I'd promised her, what she so desperately expected.

"I sensed the approach of her climax and turned so that we lay on our sides. While she shook with rapture I reached up and took hold of the end of the rod that was upon the alcohol burner. Half of it was red-hot. I removed it and at the same instant I turned myself so that Clara lay above me, my cock still buried in her pussy.

"My free hand spread her buttocks, found her anus, stretched with anticipation. In a frenzy she shook all over me, bringing us closer to our orgasm. Then, holding the rod tight, I drove it upward, never hesitating as I attained orgasm. At that instant our juices were mingling, and the smell of flesh added to my pleasure.

"Whether Clara's pleasure was greater or less, I cannot say, for when I pushed her away, she was already dead.

"Afterwards I dressed, gave some more money to the owner of the hotel, and took the next train south."

My face must have been full of disgust because he said, "No, don't look at me that way. How easy it would have been for Clara to tell the police—or anyone, in fact—about our rendezvous. How easy it would have been for her to prevent her death. But you must see, Mr. Cunningham, she wanted it to happen. She wanted to know, while at the height of her full sexual powers, what it would be like to know death in the midst of life's greatest pleasure."

Clearly, he was right, but nonetheless as maniacal as she had been, as she had always been—for even in the moments of our love, she must have known that one day she would submit herself to this outrageous experiment—he was equally mad.

"Still," I said to him, "I hold you to our agreement. Either you kill yourself or I turn you over to the police. No matter what you say, you're still a filthy murderer!"

"Must I do it at once?"

"At once! You disgust me!"

Groaning, he raised his bulk from the chair and walked up the path and into the house. I couldn't bring myself to follow him, and besides I didn't really doubt he would carry out the agreement. His reputation was everything to him.

I left my chair and walked to the gate. But as I opened it, I heard him shout, "Mr. Cunningham!"

I looked toward the house. He was at a window on the upper floor.

"It is a pity," he shouted down to me, "that death could not be as interesting for everyone as it was for Clara."

I could say nothing. I felt like a murderer—and yet this was for Arvon the lesser of two evils. Perhaps I was wrong to seat myself in judgment upon him, but how could I say—*well, all right, you old madman, go on living, go on killing madwomen*? I would have to tell the police, and in doing that, I would harm the most innocent creature of all—Angela. After all, as the only living member of this strange, doomed family she would be the one to suffer, inheriting their degradation like some dark legacy.

Arvon disappeared from the window and returned an instant later with a gun in his hand. For a moment, I thought he might take aim at me. But at last he raised it to his own temple.

"Goodbye," he shouted. "I am truly sorry to have had so much more of Clara than you."

I wanted to shout at him to stop, but instead I lowered my eyes and waited for the report. The blast was brief and much less noisy than I had expected. When I looked up I saw the enormous man swaying forward, bending deeply. Then he fell from the window, hurtled through space, and crashed into a circle of flowers at the back of the lawn.

Servants appeared from everywhere, some of them shrieking. I thought it best to slip away quietly, but then the maid who had come to the gate earlier saw me.

"What happened?" she shouted with horror.

"It was an accident."

"An accident?"

"Yes, he was going to show me that gun he has there. He lifted it to his temple jokingly. Apparently, he didn't know it was loaded. It went off and he fell out the window."

"How terrible," they all agreed and told me through their tears how he was the kindest and most generous of masters.

"Still," I consoled them, "he couldn't know what was happening. None of us could ask for a faster end."

They telephoned the police who, upon arriving, told me I'd have to stay for the inquest. This required that I spend two more days in Naire where there was absolutely nothing to do. I walked and talked to some of the locals, who developed rather a dread of me, as if I were the murderer.

At the inquest I repeated my story and I think that no one believed me. They all felt—although no one ever indicated this by word—that I was responsible for Arvon's (or Montrose's) death. The circumstances were straight enough: I appeared in Naire, to which strangers rarely come; I was admitted to the Villa Montrose, to which no one was allowed; and within two hours of all this an old, cold, but respectable man dies.

In any case, the verdict brought was accidental death. Obviously, the town would have preferred murder, suicide under compulsion, or even just plain suicide. But it was accidental death.

I left Naire twenty minutes after the verdict was announced and was back in Paris during the middle of the night. It was all over, I told myself, as I shredded Clara's list and threw the pieces away. There was only one more visit to be made.

I was certain that one would be pleasant.

202

CHAPTER
NINE

IX.

I telephoned Angela the next morning.

"Hello," she said. "I thought you'd never get in touch with me again."

"I've been busy all the time. I told you your mother had asked me to see some people."

"I know. There must have been a lot of people. Or else they had a lot to say."

"It's a bit of both, actually. You're sounding in much better spirits than the last time."

"So are you," she said.

"I confess I am in better spirits. Or I've just become so."

"And why is that?" she asked with a smile in her voice.

"Because I've been looking forward to seeing you."

"Then come at once."

"No sooner said than done."

She was waiting for me at the door of the mansion. Her dress was still one of mourning, but it was not so somber as the one she'd worn the first time we met. This one was paradoxical, for it mourned only halfway over her breasts. The fresh young mounds protruded above the cloth. The dress was of a very thin summer cloth so that through it I could see the hidden roundness of the underside of her breasts and the dark roses of her nipples. Lower down was the shadowed outline of panties clutching eagerly at her loins.

"I *am* happy to see you again," she said and put her cheek forward for a kiss, another paternal kiss.

"And I'm happy to see you."

Taking my hand, she led me into the salon, poured us each a sherry, and then sat down beside me on the sofa.

"Well," she began, "did Mother send you to see interesting people?"

"Fairly," I mumbled. "Financial men and that sort—"

"How dull for you," she smiled. "I thought Mother never bothered with those things herself."

"No, I suppose not, but—"

"And isn't it odd, but our lawyer was here just last night and said everything was all cleared up."

My embarrassment could not be hidden. "Well, the people I saw were financial people, but I saw them socially, not for any business reasons."

"I see," she said. To my astonishment she added, "You mean these were her nighttime friends."

"What are you talking about?"

"You know very well what I'm talking about!"

"I haven't the vaguest idea," I said, but the lie was evident.

"Oh, please, Howard—do you mind if I call you Howard?"

"Of course not. It pleases me." I placed my hand over hers beside me on the sofa.

"Well then, Howard, can you think it possible I've lived with a person twenty years and never noticed that she slipped out at night?"

"Perhaps she went for walks," I suggested.

"No. You know as well as I do that at night my mother was a wild woman. I've known about this ever since the war, when I was still a little girl and I met a man who had seen me walking with HER. He knew her from that terrible yacht. And he told me all about it."

"Did you tell her you knew?"

"No, never. She would have died. It would have broken her heart. As if I would have loved her less because she needed what all women need." I felt her hand tremble under mine and I put my arm around her, drawing her close.

"You're terribly sweet," I said. "How lucky Clara was to have you."

"One needn't be only Clara," she flashed, "in order to have me. But I want you to tell me something."

"What is it?"

"About Mother's death."

Indeed, I didn't dare to. "I know no more about it than you."

"Tell me, Howard…who was Serge Montrose?"

I looked at her, incredulous. "However did you hear of him?"

"There was a small item in the papers about that inquest you were a witness at. It had something to do with Mother, didn't it?"

"No, nothing at all. He was an old friend of mine."

"In the papers it said you'd never met him before and that one of the servants said they'd heard you shout something like 'Baron' at him. And he wasn't a baron, they said."

"It was a mistake."

"I don't believe you."

"It's better that you do," I said, keeping my voice even but trying to warn her it would be wiser if she asked no more questions. Yet she persisted.

"I want to know the truth. I'll bother you day and night until you tell me."

"I'd love to be bothered by you."

"Then tell me or I won't."

"All right," I said. "The details are uninteresting. But this is approximately the story: your father didn't die soon after your birth. It was a hoax."

"Did Mother know this?"

"No," I lied. "Not until the end. He sent her word of this and asked for an appointment. She was afraid he would kill her, as in fact he did."

"But why?"

"He was insane. There is no asking why. People act as they must."

"Go on."

"Well, through a series of accidents I learned of Montrose and on a hunch went to see him. It turned out he was Baron Arvon and he committed suicide rather than live to see the family name soiled if and when I told the police. I wouldn't have told the police, of course, on account of you."

She covered her face with her hands. "It's terrible. Terrible. I feel so alone."

"You're not. I'm your friend."

She looked up at me. "Yes, I believe you are."

She raised her face to mine and our lips joined. The young mouth opened to my tongue, receiving the full measure of my kiss. My hand reached over the flimsy thinness of the cloth upon her breast and I closed upon the firm flesh. Its warmth and softness yielded under my fingers and Angela sighed through the kiss.

"Let me take your dress off," I said.

"Wait." She stood up and went to the door, locking it. When she returned to me, I rose and lifted her dress, pulling it above her head. She stood before me, her pink flesh glowing, her uncovered breasts exposed to me. I cupped one in each hand, massaging them so that my fingers rubbed the tender nipples.

"How beautiful you are," I said.

She dropped her panties to the floor and I saw the luscious triangle of auburn hair.

"Please," she whispered. "You must also get undressed."

Hurriedly, I began removing my things, and as I stripped, she said, "You know, Howard, I've never seen a naked man before."

"Then look at one," I told her when my things were off.

She studied my body closely, observing my chest, my shoulders, my arms, my belly. It was an effort for her to look lower, but she did and her face pinked. Approaching me, her hand reached for my penis. She touched it lightly at first, then rubbed its underside, and at last clutched it in her hands.

"What a lovely thing," she said.

Then she put her hand under my scrotum and pushed it gently as if weighing my balls. She released them and pressed herself close to me, rubbing her belly against my cock. My hand reached down between her thighs and they opened slightly. I pushed my way in, my fingers stroking the hair, the narrow split between. A gentle moisture sprang forth as if hardly more than perspiration.

"I want to kiss you there," I said.

"I'd love you to."

We both sank to the rug. I took a head-to-foot position, hoping that I wouldn't have to ask her to suck me. I moved my head between her legs, my face joining with her pussy, rich with the smell of her womanhood. I moved my tongue slowly back and forth; she shivered and brought her thighs tight against my head. Suddenly I felt her soft lips kissing the head of my cock and I thrust at her. Her lips spread and my rod moved slowly into the warmth of her mouth.

I continued licking her, rolling my tongue again and again across her clitoris. When I brought it to the opening of her sheath, her excitement made her jump slightly. I forced my tongue through the tightness of the threshold. Her mouth was laboring passionately at my shaft, licking it up and down and swirling around the head.

"Now," I said, moving away from her.

Eyes closed, she said nothing as I drew myself up over her. I pushed her knees back and glided my cock across the moisture of her cunt. Then I aimed the head at her little hole and forced slightly, then a bit more. She moaned.

"Does it hurt?"

She shook her head. I thrust forward once more, but now the penetration could only be accomplished by a powerful lunge. I readied her by easing my cock-head in and out of the opening, and when she had begun to sigh, I pushed forward, springing the length of my member into her. I felt her maidenhead give way before my impassioned rush.

A cry broke out from her lips.

"Does it hurt?" I asked again.

"How can anything you do give me anything but pleasure?" she said softly.

I moved my penis in her, drew it half out, then once more sent it in to the hilt. This movement pleased her and I repeated it, and again, continuing with variations until suddenly she was choosing the rhythm.

My body rested upon hers and our mouths met in a long kiss, a kiss that continued through the thrusts of our loins, through the increasing pressure of excitement and our quickening movements. I felt her come close to her climax and I quickened my thrusts, making them more regular. Her teeth bit my lip; her fingers scraped across my shoulders; her legs held tight round my back. We thrust and pushed and groaned together into our orgasm. I emptied my sperm into her in three mind-numbing spurts.

"How wonderful that was," she said later.

I could only nod agreement. My hands stroked her fiery body and caressed her breasts.

"No wonder Mother loved you so much," she whispered. "Were you always so good at it?"

I smiled. "Only with a woman as wonderful as you."

"Will you always do it to me? I'll want it every minute of the day."

"Only the day? What about the nights?"

"The nights?" She laughed. "Well, Howard, I think the nights will be a mystery."

MASQUERADE BOOKS

MASQUERADE

ROBERT SEWALL
THE DEVIL'S ADVOCATE
$6.95/553-0

The return of an erotic masterpiece! The first erotic novel written and published in America, Clara Reeves appeals to Conrad Garnett, a New York district attorney, for help in tracking down her missing sister, Rita. To Clara's distress, Conrad suspects that Rita has disappeared into an unsavory underworld dominated by an illicit sex ring. Clara soon finds herself being "persuaded" to accompany Conrad on his descent into this modern-day hell, where unspeakable pleasures await....

GERALD GREY
LONDON GIRLS
$6.50/531-X

In 1875, Samuel Brown arrived in London, determined to take the glorious city by storm. And sure enough, Samuel quickly distinguishes himself as one of the city's most notorious rakehells. Young Mr. Brown knows well the many ways of making a lady weak at the knees—and uses them not only to his delight, but to his enormous profit! A rollicking tale of cosmopolitan lust.

OLIVIA M. RAVENSWORTH
THE DESIRES OF REBECCA
$6.50/532-8

A swashbuckling tale of lesbian desire in Merrie Olde England. Beautiful Rebecca follows her passions from the simple love of the girl next door to the relentless lechery of London's most notorious brothel, hoping for the ultimate thrill. Finally, she casts her lot with a crew of saphic buccaneers, each of whom is more than capable of matching Rebecca lust for lust....

ATAULLAH MARDAAN
KAMA HOURI/DEVA DASI
$7.95/512-3

"...memorable for the author's ability to evoke India present and past.... Mardaan excels in crowding her pages with the sights and smells of India, and her erotic descriptions are convincingly realistic."
—Michael Perkins,
The Secret Record: Modern Erotic Literature
Two legendary tales of the East in one spectacular volume. *Kama Houri* details the life of a sheltered Western woman who finds herself living within the confines of a harem—where she discovers herself thrilled with the extent of her servitude. *Deva Dasi* is a tale dedicated to the cult of the Dasis—the sacred women of India who devoted their lives to the fulfillment of the senses—while revealing the sexual rites of Shiva. A special double volume.

J. P. KANSAS
ANDREA AT THE CENTER
$6.50/498-4

Kidnapped! Lithe and lovely young Andrea is whisked away to a distant retreat. Gradually, she is introduced to the ways of the Center, and soon becomes quite friendly with its other inhabitants—all of whom are learning to abandon restraint in their pursuit of the deepest sexual satisfaction. Soon, Andrea takes her place as one of the Center's greatest success stories—a submissive seductress who answers to any and all! A nationally bestselling title, and one of modern erotica's true classics.

VISCOUNT LADYWOOD
GYNECOCRACY
$9.95/511-5

An infamous story of female domination returns to print. Julian, whose parents feel he shows just a bit too much spunk, is sent to a very special private school, in hopes that he will learn to discipline his wayward soul. Once there, Julian discovers that his program of study has been devised by the deliciously stern Mademoiselle de Chambonnard. In no time, Julian is learning the many ways of pleasure and pain—under the firm hand of this beautifully demanding headmistress.

CHARLOTTE ROSE, EDITOR
THE 50 BEST PLAYGIRL FANTASIES
$6.50/460-7

A steamy selection of women's fantasies straight from the pages of *Playgirl*—the leading magazine of sexy entertainment for women. These tales of seduction—specially selected by no less an authority than Charlotte Rose, author of such bestselling women's erotica as *Women at Work* and *The Doctor is In*—are sure to set your pulse racing.

N. T. MORLEY
THE CASTLE
$6.95/530-1

A pulse-pounding peek into the ultimate vacation paradise—a secret world where carnal delights of every sort await those intrepid enough to explore the shadows of their own souls. Tess Roberts is held captive by a crew of disciplinarians intent on making all her dreams come true. While anyone can arrange for a stay at the Castle, Tess proves herself one of the most gifted applicants yet....

THE PARLOR
$6.50/496-8

Lovely Kathryn gives in to the ultimate temptation. The mysterious John and Sarah ask her to be their slave—an idea that turns Kathryn on so much that she can't refuse! But who are these two mysterious strangers? Little by little, Kathryn not only learns to serve, but comes to know the inner secrets of her stunning keepers.

MASQUERADE BOOKS

J. A. GUERRA, EDITOR

COME QUICKLY:
For Couples on the Go
$6.50/461-5
The increasing pace of daily life is no reason to forgo a little carnal pleasure whenever the mood strikes. Here are over sixty of the hottest fantasies around—all designed to get you going in less time than it takes to dial 976. A super-hot volume especially for modern couples on a hectic schedule.

ERICA BRONTE

LUST, INC.
$6.50/467-4
Lust, Inc. explores the extremes of passion that lurk beneath even the coldest, most businesslike exteriors. Join in the sexy escapades of a group of high-powered professionals whose idea of office decorum is like nothing you've ever encountered! Business attire is decidedly not required for this look at high-powered sexual negotiations!

VANESSA DURIÈS

THE TIES THAT BIND
$6.50/510-7
The incredible confessions of a thrillingly unconventional woman. From the first page, this chronicle of dominance and submission will keep you gasping with its vivid depictions of sensual abandon. At the hand of Masters Georges, Patrick, Pierre and others, this submissive seductress experiences pleasures she never knew existed.... One of modern erotica's best-selling accounts of real-life dominance and submission.

M. S. VALENTINE

ELYSIAN DAYS AND NIGHTS
$6.95/536-0
From around the world, the most beautiful—and wealthy—neglected young wives arrive at the Elysian Spa intent on receiving a little heavy-duty pampering. Luckily, the spa's proprietor is a true devotee of the female form—and has dedicated himself and his staff to the pure pleasure of every lovely lady who crosses Elysium's threshold....

THE CAPTIVITY OF CELIA
$6.50/453-4
Colin is considered the prime suspect in a murder, forcing him to seek refuge with his cousin, Sir Jason Hardwicke. In exchange for Colin's safety, Jason demands Celia's unquestioning submission.... Sexual extortion guarantees her lover's safety—as well as provide Celia with ever mor exciting sensual delights. Soon, she finds herself entranced by the demands of her captor....

AMANDA WARE

BINDING CONTRACT
$6.50/491-7
Louise was responsible for bringing many prestigious clients into Claremont's salon—so he was more than willing to have her miss a little work in order to pleasure one of his most important customers. But Eleanor Cavendish had her mind set on something more rigorous than a simple wash and set. Sexual slavery!

BOUND TO THE PAST
$6.50/452-6
Anne accepts a research assignment in a Tudor mansion. Upon arriving, she finds herself aroused by James, a descendant of the mansion's owners. Together they uncover the perverse desires of the mansion's long-dead master—desires that bind Anne inexorably to the past—not to mention the bedpost!

SACHI MIZUNO

SHINJUKU NIGHTS
$6.50/493-3
A tour through the lives and libidos of the seductive East. No one is better that Sachi Mizuno at weaving an intricate web of sensual desire, wherein many characters are ensnared and enraptured by the demands of their carnal natures.

PASSION IN TOKYO
$6.50/454-2
Tokyo—one of Asia's most historic and seductive cities. Come behind the closed doors of its citizens, and witness the many pleasures that await. Lusty men and women from every stratum of society free themselves of all inhibitions....

MARTINE GLOWINSKI

POINT OF VIEW
$6.50/433-X
The story of one woman's extraordinary erotic awakening. With the assistance of her new, unexpectedly kinky lover, she discovers and explores her exhibitionist tendencies—until there is virtually nothing she won't do before the horny audiences her man arranges! Unabashed acting out for the sophisticated voyeur.

RICHARD McGOWAN

A HARLOT OF VENUS
$6.50/425-9
A highly fanciful, epic tale of lust on Mars! Cavortia—the most famous and sought-after courtesan in the cosmopolitan city of Venus—finds love and much more during her adventures with some of the most remarkable characters in recent erotic fiction.

MASQUERADE BOOKS

CAROLE REMY

FANTASY IMPROMPTU
$6.50/513-1
Kidnapped and held in a remote island retreat, Chantal—a renowned erotic writer—finds herself catering to every sexual whim of the mysterious and arousing Bran. Bran is determined to bring Chantal to a full embracing of her sensual nature, even while revealing himself to be something far more than human....

BEAUTY OF THE BEAST
$5.95/332-5
A shocking tell-all, written from the point-of-view of a prize-winning reporter. And what reporting she does! All the secrets of an uninhibited life are revealed, and each lusty tableau is painted in glowing colors.

DAVID AARON CLARK

THE MARQUIS DE SADE'S JULIETTE
$4.95/240-X
The Marquis de Sade's infamous Juliette returns—and emerges as the most perverse and destructive nightstalker modern New York will ever know. One by one, the innocent are drawn in by Juliette's empty promise of immortality, only to fall prey to her deadly lusts.

ANONYMOUS

LOVE'S ILLUSION
$6.95/549-2
Elizabeth Renard yearned for the body of rich and successful Dan Harrington. Then she discovered Harrington's secret weakness: a need to be humiliated and punished. She makes him her slave, and together they commence a journey into depravity that leaves nothing to the imagination—nothing!

NADIA
$5.95/267-1
Follow the delicious but neglected Nadia as she works to wring every drop of pleasure out of life—despite an unhappy marriage. A classic title providing a peek into the secret sexual lives of another time and place.

NIGEL McPARR

THE TRANSFORMATION OF EMILY
$6.50/519-0
The shocking story of Emily Johnson, live-in domestic. Without warning, Emily finds herself dismissed by her mistress, and sent to serve at Lilac Row—the home of Charles and Harriet Godwin. In no time, Harriet has Emily doing things she'd never dreamed would be required of her—all involving shocking erotic discipline.

TITIAN BERESFORD

CINDERELLA
$6.50/500-X
Beresford triumphs again with this intoxicating tale, filled with castle dungeons and tightly corseted ladies-in-waiting, naughty viscounts and impossibly cruel masturbatrixes—nearly every conceivable method of erotic torture is explored and described in lush, vivid detail.

JUDITH BOSTON
$6.50/525-5
Edward would have been lucky to get the stodgy companion he thought his parents had hired for him. But an exquisite woman arrives at his door, and Edward finds his lewd behavior never goes unpunished by the unflinchingly severe Judith Boston

NINA FOXTON
$5.95/443-7
An aristocrat finds herself bored by run-of-the-mill amusements for "ladies of good breeding." Instead of taking tea with proper gentlemen, naughty Nina "milks" them of their most private essences. No man ever says "No" to Nina!

P. N. DEDEAUX

THE NOTHING THINGS
$5.95/404-6
Beta Beta Rho has taken on a new group of pledges. The five women will be put through the most grueling of ordeals, and punished severely for any shortcomings. Before long, all Beta pledges come to crave their punishments—and eagerly await next year's crop! Sex-crazed coeds defile every virgin in sight!

LYN DAVENPORT

THE GUARDIAN II
$6.50/505-0
The tale of submissive Felicia Brookes continues in this volume of sensual surprises. No sooner has Felicia come to love Rodney than she discovers that she must now accustom herself to the guardianship of the debauched Duke of Smithton. Surely Rodney will rescue her from the domination of this stranger. Won't he?

DOVER ISLAND
$5.95/384-8
On a island off the west coast, Dr. David Kelly has planted the seeds of his dream—a Corporal Punishment Resort. Soon, many people from varied walks of life descend upon this isolated retreat, intent on fulfilling their every desire. Including Marcy Harris, the perfect partner for the lustful Doctor....

BUY ANY 4 BOOKS & CHOOSE 1 ADDITIONAL BOOK, OF EQUAL OR LESSER VALUE, AS YOUR FREE GIFT

MASQUERADE BOOKS

LIZBETH DUSSEAU

THE APPLICANT
$6.50/501-8

"Adventuresome young women who enjoys being submissive sought by married couple in early forties. Expect no limits." Hilary answers an ad, hoping to find someone who can meet her special needs. The beautiful Liza turns out to be a flawless mistress, and together with her husband, Oliver, she trains Hilary to be the perfect servant—much to Hilary's delight and arousal!

ANTHONY BOBARZYNSKI

STASI SLUT
$4.95/3050-4

Adina lives in East Germany, where she can only dream about the freedoms of the West. But then she meets a group of ruthless and corrupt STASI agents. They use her body for their own perverse gratification, while she opts to use her talents in a final bid for total freedom!

JOCELYN JOYCE

PRIVATE LIVES
$4.95/309-0

The lecherous habits of the illustrious make for a sizzling tale of French erotic life. A widow has a craving for a young busboy; he's sleeping with a rich businessman's wife; her husband is minding his sex business elsewhere! Sexual entanglements run through this tale of upper crust lust!

SARAH JACKSON

SANCTUARY
$5.95/318-X

Sanctuary explores both the unspeakable debauchery of court life and the unimaginable privations of monastic solitude, leading the voracious and the virtuous on a collision course that brings history to throbbing life.

THE WILD HEART
$4.95/3007-5

A luxury hotel is the setting for this artful web of sex, desire, and love. A newlywed sees sex as a duty, while her hungry husband tries to awaken her to its tender joys. A Parisian entertains wealthy guests for the love of money. Each episode provides a perverse new variation in this lusty Grand Hotel!

SARA H. FRENCH

MASTER OF TIMBERLAND
$5.95/327-9

A tale of sexual slavery at the ultimate paradise resort—where sizzling submissives serve their masters without question. One of our bestselling titles, this trek to Timberland has ignited desires the world over—and stands poised to become one of modern erotica's legendary tales.

MARY LOVE

ANGELA
$6.95/545-X

Angela's game is "look but don't touch," and she drives everyone mad with desire, dancing for their pleasure but never allowing a single caress. Soon her sensual spell is cast, and she's the only one who can break it! Watch as she finally throws herself open to the world!

MASTERING MARY SUE
$5.95/351-1

Mary Sue is a rich nymphomaniac whose husband is determined to declare her mentally incompetent and gain control of her fortune. He brings her to a castle where, to Mary Sue's delight, she is unleashed for a veritable sex-fest!

THE BEST OF MARY LOVE
$4.95/3099-7

Mary Love leaves no coupling untried and no extreme unexplored in these scandalous selections from *Mastering Mary Sue, Ecstasy on Fire, Vice Park Place, Wanda,* and *Naughtier at Night.*

AMARANTHA KNIGHT

The Darker Passions: THE PICTURE OF DORIAN GRAY
$6.50/342-2

Amarantha Knight takes on Oscar Wilde, resulting in a fabulously decadent tale of highly personal changes. One young woman finds her most secret desires laid bare by a portrait far more revealing than she could have imagined. Soon she benefits from a skillful masquerade.

THE DARKER PASSIONS READER
$6.50/432-1

The best moments from Knight's phenomenally popular Darker Passions series. Here are the most eerily erotic passages from her acclaimed sexual reworkings of *Dracula, Frankenstein, Dr. Jekyll & Mr. Hyde* and *The Fall of the House of Usher.*

The Darker Passions: THE FALL OF THE HOUSE OF USHER
$6.50/528-X

Two weary travelers arrive at a dark and foreboding mansion, where they fall victim to the many bizarre appetites of its residents. The Master and Mistress of the house of Usher indulge in every form of decadence, and initiate their guests into the many pleasures to be found in utter submission.

The Darker Passions: DR. JEKYLL AND MR. HYDE
$4.95/227-2

It is a story of incredible transformations achieved through mysterious experiments. Explore the steamy possibilities of a tale where no one is quite who—or what—they seem. Victorian bedrooms explode with hidden demons!

MASQUERADE BOOKS

The Darker Passions: FRANKENSTEIN
$5.95/248-5

What if you could create a living human? What shocking acts could it be taught to perform, to desire? Find out what pleasures await those who play God....

The Darker Passions: DRACULA
$5.95/326-0

"Well-written and imaginative, Amarantha Knight gives fresh impetus to this myth, taking us through the sexual and sadistic scenes with details that keep us reading.... A classic in itself has been added to the shelves."   —*Divinity*

The infamous erotic retelling of the Vampire legend.

THE PAUL LITTLE LIBRARY
LOVE SLAVE/PECULIAR PASSIONS OF LADY MEG
$8.95/529-8/Trade paperback

Two classics from erotica's most popular author! What does it take to be the perfect instrument of pleasure—or go about acquiring a willing *Love Slave* of one's own? What are the appetites that lurk beneath *Lady Meg*? Paul Little spares no detail in these two relentless tales!

CELESTE
$6.95/544-1

It's definitely all in the family for this female duo of sexual dynamics. While traveling through Europe, these two try everything and everyone on their hrony holiday. These two will try anything—including each other!

ALL THE WAY
$6.95/509-3

Two excruciating novels from Paul Little in one hot volume! *Going All the Way* features an unhappy man who tries to purge himself of the memory of his lover with a series of quirky and uninhibited lovers. *Pushover* tells the story of a serial spanker and his celebrated exploits.

THE DISCIPLINE OF ODETTE
$5.95/334-1

Odette was sure marriage would rescue her from her family's "corrections." To her horror, she discovers that her beloved has also been raised on discipline. A shocking erotic coupling!

THE END OF INNOCENCE
$6.95/546-8

The early days of Women's Emancipation are the setting for this story of some very independent ladies. These women were willing to go to any lengths to fight for their sexual freedom, and willing to endure any punishment in their desire for total liberation.

TUTORED IN LUST
$6.95/547-6

This tale of the initiation and instruction of a carnal college co-ed and her fellow students unlocks the sex secrets of the classroom.

THE BEST OF PAUL LITTLE
$6.50/469-0

Known for his fantastic portrayals of punishment and pleasure, Little never fails to push readers over the edge of sensual excitement.

THE PRISONER
$5.95/330-9

Judge Black has built a secret room below a penitentiary, where he sentences the prisoners to hours of exhibition and torment while his friends watch. Judge Black's brand of rough justice keeps his lovely captives on the brink of utter pleasure!

TEARS OF THE INQUISITION
$4.95/146-2

A staggering account of pleasure and punishment. "There was a tickling inside her as her nervous system reminded her she was ready for sex. But before her was...the Inquisitor!"

DOUBLE NOVEL
$4.95/86-6

The Metamorphosis of Lisette Joyaux tells the story of a young woman initiated into an incredible world world of lesbian lusts. *The Story of Monique* reveals the twisted sexual rituals that beckon the ripe and willing Monique.

CAPTIVE MAIDENS
$5.95/440-2

Three beautiful young women find themselves powerless against the debauched landowners of 1824 England. They are banished to a sex colony, and corrupted by every imaginable perversion.

SLAVE ISLAND
$5.95/441-0

A leisure cruise is waylaid by Lord Henry Philbrock, a sadistic genius. The ship's passengers are kidnapped and spirited to his island prison, where the women are trained to accommodate the most bizarre sexual cravings of the rich, the famous, the pampered and the perverted.

ALIZARIN LAKE
CLARA
$6.95/548-4

The mysterious death of a beautiful woman leads her old boyfriend on a harrowing journey of discovery. His search uncovers a woman on a quest for deeper and more unusual sensations, each more shocking than the one before!

MASQUERADE BOOKS

SEX ON DOCTOR'S ORDERS
$5.95/402-X
Beth, a nubile young nurse, uses her considerable skills to further medical science by offering incomparable and insatiable assistance in the gathering of important specimens.

THE EROTIC ADVENTURES OF HARRY TEMPLE
$4.95/127-6
Harry Temple's memoirs chronicle his amorous adventures from his initiation at the hands of insatiable sirens, through his stay at a house of hot repute, to his encounters with a chastity-belted nympho!

JOHN NORMAN

TARNSMAN OF GOR
$6.95/486-0
This controversial series returns! Tarl Cabot is transported to Gor. He must quickly accustom himself to the ways of this world, including the caste system which exalts some as Priest-Kings or Warriors, and debases others as slaves.

OUTLAW OF GOR
$6.95/487-9
Tarl Cabot returns to Gor, to reclaim both his woman and his role of Warrior. But upon arriving, he discovers that his name, his city and the names of those he loves have become unspeakable. Cabot has become an outlaw, and must discover his new purpose on this strange planet, where danger stalks the outcast, and even simple answers have their price....

PRIEST-KINGS OF GOR
$6.95/488-7
Tarl Cabot searches for his lovely wife Talena. Does she live, or was she destroyed by the all-powerful Priest-Kings? Cabot is determined to find out—even while knowing that no one who has approached the mountain stronghold of the Priest-Kings has ever returned alive....

NOMADS OF GOR
$6.95/527-1
Norman's heroic Tarnsman finds his way across this Counter-Earth, pledged to serve the Priest-Kings in their quest for survival. Unfortunately for Cabot, his mission leads him to the savage Wagon People—nomads who may very well kill before surrendering any secrets....

ASSASSIN OF GOR
$6.95/538-7
Assassin of Gor exposes the brutal caste system of Gor at its most unsparing: from the Assassin Kuurus, on a mission of bloody vengeance, to Pleasure Slaves, tirelessly trained in the ways of personal ecstasy. From one social stratum to the next, the inhabitants of Counter-Earth pursue and are pursued by all-too human passions—and the inescapable destinies that await their caste...

SYDNEY ST. JAMES

RIVE GAUCHE
$5.95/317-1
The Latin Quarter, Paris, circa 1920. Expatriate bohemians couple with abandon—before eventually abandoning their ambitions amidst the intoxicating temptations waiting to be indulged in every bedroom.

GARDEN OF DELIGHT
$4.95/3058-X
A vivid account of sexual awakening that follows an innocent but insatiably curious young woman's journey from the furtive, forbidden joys of dormitory life to the unabashed carnality of the wild world.

DON WINSLOW

THE FALL OF THE ICE QUEEN
$6.50/520-4
She was the most exquisite of his courtiers: the beautiful, aloof woman who Rahn the Conqueror chose as his Consort. But the regal disregard with which she treated Rahn was not to be endured. It was decided that she would submit to his will, and learn to serve her lord in the fashion he had come to expect. And as so many had learned, Rahn's depraved expectations have made his court infamous....

PRIVATE PLEASURES
$6.50/504-2
An assortment of sensual encounters designed to appeal to the most discerning reader. Frantic voyeurs, licentious exhibitionists, and everyday lovers are here displayed in all their wanton glory—proving again that fleshly pleasures have no more apt chronicler than Don Winslow.

THE INSATIABLE MISTRESS OF ROSEDALE
$6.50/494-1
The story of the perfect couple: Edward and Lady Penelope, who reside in beautiful and mysterious Rosedale manor. While Edward is a true connoisseur of sexual perversion, it is Lady Penelope whose mastery of complete sensual pleasure makes their home infamous. Indulging one another's bizarre whims is a way of life for this wicked couple, and none who encounter the extravagances of Rosedale will forget what they've learned....

SECRETS OF CHEATEM MANOR
$6.50/434-8
Edward returns to his late father's estate, to find it being run by the majestic Lady Amanda. Edward can hardly believe his luck—Lady Amanda is assisted by her two beautiful, lonely daughters, Catherine and Prudence. What the randy young man soon comes to realize is the love of discipline that all three beauties share.

MASQUERADE BOOKS

KATERINA IN CHARGE
$5.95/409-7

When invited to a country retreat by a mysterious couple, two randy young ladies can hardly resist! But do they have any idea what they're in for? Whatever the case, the imperious Katerina will make her desires known very soon— and demand that they be fulfilled… A thoroughly perverse tale of ultimate sexual innocence subjugated and defiled by one powerful woman.

THE MANY PLEASURES OF IRONWOOD
$5.95/310-4

Seven lovely young women are employed by The Ironwood Sportsmen's Club, where their natural talents in the sensual arts are put to creative use. A small and exclusive club with seven carefully selected sexual connoisseurs, Ironwood is dedicated to the relentless pursuit of forbidden pleasures.

CLAIRE'S GIRLS
$5.95/442-9

You knew when she walked by that she was something special. She was one of Claire's girls, a woman carefully dressed and groomed to fill a role, to capture a look, to fit an image crafted by the sophisticated proprietress of an exclusive escort agency. High-class whores blow the roof off in this blow-by-blow account of life behind the closed doors of a brothel.

N. WHALLEN

TAU'TEVU
$6.50/426-7

In a mysterious and exotic land, the statuesque and beautiful Vivian learns to subject herself to the hand of a strange and domineering man. He systematically helps her prove her own strength, and brings to life in her an unimagined sensual fire.

THE CLASSIC COLLECTION
PROTESTS, PLEASURES, RAPTURES
$5.95/400-3

Invited for an allegedly quiet weekend at a country vicarage, a young woman is stunned to find herself surrounded by shocking acts of sexual sadism. Soon her curiosity is piqued, and she begins to explore her own capacities for delicious sexual cruelty.

THE YELLOW ROOM
$5.95/378-3

The "yellow room" holds the secrets of lust, lechery, and the lash. There, bare-bottomed, spread-eagled, and open to the world, demure Alice Darvell soon learns to love her lickings.

SCHOOL DAYS IN PARIS
$5.95/325-2

Few Universities provide the profound and pleasurable lessons one learns in after-hours study—particularly if one is young and available, and lucky enough to have Paris as a playground.

MAN WITH A MAID
$4.95/307-4

The adventures of Jack and Alice have delighted readers for eight decades! A classic of its genre, *Man with a Maid* tells a tale of desire, revenge, and submission. Over 200,000 copies in print!

CLASSIC EROTIC BIOGRAPHIES

JENNIFER III
$5.95/292-2

The adventures of erotica's most daring heroine. Jennifer has a photographer's eye for details—particularly of the male variety! One by one, her subjects submit to her demands for pleasure.

RHINOCEROS

KATHLEEN K.

SWEET TALKERS
$6.95/516-6

"If you enjoy eavesdropping on explicit conversations about sex... this book is for you."
—*Spectator*

Kathleen K. ran a phone-sex company in the late 80s, and she opens up her diary for a very thought provoking peek at the life of a phone-sex operator. Transcripts of actual conversations are included.
Trade /$12.95/192-6

THOMAS S. ROCHE

DARK MATTER
$6.95/484-4

"*Dark Matter* is sure to please gender outlaws, bodymod junkies, goth vampires, boys who wish they were dykes, and anybody who's not to sure where the fine line should be drawn between pleasure and pain. It's a handful."—Pat Califia

"Here is the erotica of the cumming millennium.… You will be deliciously disturbed, but never disappointed."
—Poppy Z. Brite

NOIROTICA: An Anthology of Erotic Crime Stories (Ed.)
$6.95/390-2

A collection of darkly sexy tales, taking place at the crossroads of the crime and erotic genres. Here are some of today's finest writers of sexual fiction, all of whom explore the murky terrain where desire runs irrevocably afoul of the law.

BUY ANY 4 BOOKS & CHOOSE 1 ADDITIONAL BOOK, OF EQUAL OR LESSER VALUE, AS YOUR FREE GIFT

MASQUERADE BOOKS

ROMY ROSEN

SPUNK
$6.95/492-5

Casey, a lovely model poised upon the verge of super-celebrity, falls for an insatiable young rock singer—not suspecting that his sexual appetite has led him to experiment with a dangerous new aphrodisiac. Soon, Casey becomes addicted to the drug, and her craving plunges her into a strange underworld, where the only chance for redemption lies with a shadowy young man with a secret of his own.

MOLLY WEATHERFIELD

CARRIE'S STORY
$6.95/485-2

"I was stunned by how well it was written and how intensely foreign I found its sexual world.... And, since this is a world I don't frequent... I thoroughly enjoyed the National Geo tour."
—*bOING bOING*

"Hilarious and harrowing... just when you think things can't get any wilder, they do."
—*Black Sheets*

"I had been Jonathan's slave for about a year when he told me he wanted to sell me at an auction. I wasn't in any condition to respond when he told me this…" Desire and depravity run rampant in this story of uncompromising mastery and irrevocable submission. A unique piece of erotica that is both thoughtful and hot!

CYBERSEX CONSORTIUM

CYBERSEX: The Perv's Guide to Finding Sex on the Internet
$6.95/471-2

You've heard the objections: cyberspace is soaked with sex, mired in immorality. Okay—so where is it!? Tracking down the good stuff—the real good stuff—can waste an awful lot of expensive time, and frequently leave you high and dry. The Cybersex Consortium presents an easy-to-use guide for those intrepid adults who know what they want. No horny hacker can afford to pass up this map to the kinkiest rest stops on the Info Superhighway.

AMELIA G, EDITOR

BACKSTAGE PASSES
$6.95/438-0

Amelia G, editor of the goth-sex journal *Blue Blood*, has brought together some of today's most irreverent writers, each of whom has outdone themselves with an edgy, antic tale of modern lust. Punks, metalheads, and grunge-trash roam the pages of *Backstage Passes*, and no one knows their ways better...

GERI NETTICK WITH BETH ELLIOT

MIRRORS: Portrait of a Lesbian Transsexual
$6.95/435-6

The alternately heartbreaking and empowering story of one woman's long road to full selfhood. Born a male, Geri Nettick knew something just didn't fit. And even after coming to terms with her own gender dysphoria—and taking steps to correct it—she still fought to be accepted by the lesbian feminist community to which she felt she belonged. A true tale of struggle and discovery.

DAVID MELTZER

UNDER
$6.95/290-6

The story of a 21st century sex professional living at the bottom of the social heap. After surgeries designed to increase his physical allure, corrupt government forces drive the cyber-gigolo underground—where even more bizarre cultures await him.

ORF
$6.95/110-1

He is the ultimate musician-hero—the idol of thousands, the fevered dream of many more. And like many musicians before him, he is misunderstood, misused—and totally out of control. Every last drop of feeling is squeezed from a modern-day troubadour and his lady love.

LAURA ANTONIOU, EDITOR

NO OTHER TRIBUTE
$6.95/294-9

A collection sure to challenge Political Correctness in a way few have before, with tales of women kept in bondage to their lovers by their deepest passions. Love pushes these women beyond acceptable limits, rendering them helpless to deny anything to the men and women they adore.

SOME WOMEN
$6.95/300-7

Over forty essays written by women actively involved in consensual dominance and submission. Pro doms, lifestyle leatherdykes, titleholders—women from every walk of life lay bare their true feelings about explosive issues.

BY HER SUBDUED
$6.95/281-7

These tales all involve women in control—of their lives, their loves, their men. So much in control that they can remorselessly break rules to become powerful goddesses of the men who sacrifice all to worship at their feet.

MASQUERADE BOOKS

TRISTAN TAORMINO & DAVID AARON CLARK, EDS.
RITUAL SEX
$6.95/391-0

The many contributors to *Ritual Sex* know—and demonstrate—that body and soul share more common ground than society feels comfortable acknowledging. From memoirs of ecstatic revelation, to quests to reconcile sex and spirit, *Ritual Sex* provides an unprecedented look at private life.

TAMMY JO ECKHART
AMAZONS: Erotic Explorations of Ancient Myths
$7.95/534-4

The Amazon—the fierce, independent woman warrior—appears in the traditions of many cultures, but never before has the full erotic potential of this archetype been explored with such imagination and energy. Powerful pleasures await anyone lucky enough to encounter Eckhart's legendary spitfires.

PUNISHMENT FOR THE CRIME
$6.95/427-5

Peopled by characters of rare depth, these stories explore the true meaning of dominance and submission. From an encounter between two of society's most despised individuals, to the explorations of longtime friends, these tales take you where few others have ever dared....

AMARANTHA KNIGHT, ED.
SEDUCTIVE SPECTRES
$6.95/464-X

Breathtaking tours through the erotic supernatural via the imaginations of today's best writers. Never have ghostly encounters been so alluring, thanks to a cast of otherworldly characters well-acquainted with the pleasures of the flesh.

SEX MACABRE
$6.95/392-9

Horror tales designed for dark and sexy nights. Amarantha Knight—the woman behind the Darker Passions series—has gathered together erotic stories sure to make your skin crawl, and heart beat faster.

FLESH FANTASTIC
$6.95/352-X

Humans have long toyed with the idea of "playing God": creating life from nothingness, bringing life to the inanimate. Now Amarantha Knight collects stories exploring not only the act of Creation, but the lust that follows. Includes work by some of today's edgiest writers.

GARY BOWEN
DIARY OF A VAMPIRE
$6.95/331-7

"Gifted with a darkly sensual vision and a fresh voice, [Bowen] is a writer to watch out for."   —Cecilia Tan

Rafael, a red-blooded male with an insatiable hunger for the same, is the perfect antidote to the effete malcontents haunting bookstores today. The emergence of a bold and brilliant vision, rooted in past and present.

RENÉ MAIZEROY
FLESHLY ATTRACTIONS
$6.95/299-X

Lucien was the son of the wantonly beautiful actress, Marie-Rose Hardanges. When she decides to let a "friend" introduce her son to the pleasures of love, Marie-Rose could not have foretold the excesses that would lead to her own ruin and that of her cherished son.

JEAN STINE
THRILL CITY
$6.95/411-9

Thrill City is the seat of the world's increasing depravity, and this classic novel transports you there with a vivid style you'd be hard pressed to ignore. No writer is better suited to describe the extremes of this modern Babylon.

SEASON OF THE WITCH
$6.95/268-X

"A future in which it is technically possible to transfer the total mind...of a rapist killer into the brain dead but physically living body of his female victim. Remarkable for intense psychological technique. There is eroticism but it is necessary to mark the differences between the sexes and the subtle altering of a man into a woman."   —*The Science Fiction Critic*

GRANT ANTREWS
ROGUES GALLERY
$6.95/522-0

A stirring evocation of dominant/submissive love. Two doctors meet and slowly fall in love. Once Beth reveals her hidden desires to Jim, the two explore the forbidden acts that will come to define their distinctly exotic affair.

JOHN WARREN
THE TORQUEMADA KILLER
$6.95/367-8

Detective Eva Hernandez gets her first "big case": a string of vicious murders taking place within New York's SM community. Eva assembles the evidence, revealing a picture of a world misunderstood and under attack—and gradually comes to understand her own place within it.

BUY ANY 4 BOOKS & CHOOSE 1 ADDITIONAL BOOK, OF EQUAL OR LESSER VALUE, AS YOUR FREE GIFT

MASQUERADE BOOKS

PHILIP JOSÉ FARMER
A FEAST UNKNOWN
$6.95/276-0

"Sprawling, brawling, shocking, suspenseful, hilarious…"
—Theodore Sturgeon

Farmer's supreme anti-hero returns. "I was conceived and born in 1888." Slowly, Lord Grandrith—armed with the belief that he is the son of Jack the Ripper—tells the story of his remarkable and unbridled life. His story begins with his discovery of the secret of immortality—and progresses to encompass the furthest extremes of human behavior.

SAMUEL R. DELANY
THE MAD MAN
$8.99/408-9

"Reads like a pornographic reflection of Peter Ackroyd's Chatterton or A. S. Byatt's Possession…. Delany develops an insightful dichotomy between [his protagonist]'s two worlds: the one of cerebral philosophy and dry academia, the other of heedless, 'impersonal' obsessive sexual extremism. When these worlds finally collide…the novel achieves a surprisingly satisfying resolution…."
—Publishers Weekly

Graduate student John Marr researches the life of Timothy Hasler: a philosopher whose career was cut tragically short over a decade earlier. On another front, Marr finds himself increasingly drawn toward shocking, depraved sexual entanglements with the homeless men of his neighborhood, until it begins to seem that Hasler's death might hold some key to his own life as a gay man in the age of AIDS. Unquestionably one of Samuel R. Delany's most challenging novels, and a must for any reader concerned with the state of the erotic in modern literature.

ANDREI CODRESCU
THE REPENTANCE OF LORRAINE
$6.95/329-5

"One of our most prodigiously talented and magical writers."
—NYT Book Review

By the acclaimed author of *The Hole in the Flag* and *The Blood Countess*. An aspiring writer, a professor's wife, a secretary, gold anklets, Maoists, Roman harlots—and more—swirl through this spicy tale of a harried quest for a mythic artifact. Written when the author was a young man, this lusty yarn was inspired by the heady days of the Sixties. Includes a new introduction by the author, detailing the events that inspired *Lorraine's* creation. A touching, arousing product from a more innocent time.

TUPPY OWENS
SENSATIONS
$6.95/3081-4

Tuppy Owens tells the unexpurgated story of the making of *Sensations*—the first big-budget sex flick. Originally commissioned to appear in book form after the release of the film in 1975, *Sensations* is finally released under Masquerade's stylish Rhinoceros imprint. A rare peek behind the scenes of a porn-flick, from the genre's early, groundbreaking days.

SOPHIE GALLEYMORE BIRD
MANEATER
$6.95/103-9

Through a bizarre act of creation, a man attains the "perfect" lover—by all appearances a beautiful, sensuous woman, but in reality something far darker. Once brought to life she will accept no mate, seeking instead the prey that will sate her hunger for vengeance. A biting take on the war of the sexes.

LEOPOLD VON SACHER-MASOCH
VENUS IN FURS
$6.95/3089-X

The first uncompromising exploration of the dominant/submissive relationship in literature. The alliance of Severin and Wanda epitomizes Sacher-Masoch's dark obsession with a cruel, controlling goddess and the urges that drive the man held in her thrall.

BADBOY

BARRY ALEXANDER
ALL THE RIGHT PLACES
$6.95/482-8

Stories filled with hot studs in lust and love. From modern masters and slaves to medieval royals and their subjects, Alexander explores the mating rituals men have engaged in for centuries—all in the name of sometimes hidden desires…

MICHAEL FORD, EDITOR
BUTCHBOYS:
Stories For Men Who Need It Bad
$6.50/523-9

A big volume of tales dedicated to the rough-and-tumble type who can make a man weak at the knees. Some of today's best erotic writers explore the many possible variations on the age-old fantasy of the dominant man.

BUY ANY 4 BOOKS & CHOOSE 1 ADDITIONAL BOOK, OF EQUAL OR LESSER VALUE, AS YOUR FREE GIFT